Pony Tails

For Keziah –

Pony Tails

SUSAN JAMESON

with love from

Sue xx

Forelock Books

Published by Forelock Books Ltd.

Beaglejack Barn, Blackgate Lane, Pulborough,
West Sussex. RH20 1DD

www.forelock-books.co.uk

First published in 2014

Printed in the EU on behalf of Latitude Press Ltd.
Typeset by LKSDesigns.co.uk

A CIP catalogue record for this book is available from the British Library

ISBN 978-0-9928708-5-0

In memory of Perilla of Greenlease
- a very small pony with a very big heart

Contents

The Connemara

The Connemara

"Where are my other jodhpurs? I specially left them on the stairs! Why can't you leave things alone, Rosie? Dad, she's moved them!"

"I haven't touched them. And anyway, why would I want your smelly jodhpurs? Yuk! The only thing worse would be a pair of your smelly..."

"That's enough!" Dad appeared at the bottom of the staircase, his arms piled up with jackets and tickets and maps. His daughters mostly got on well together, but journeys seemed to bring out the worst in them. They weren't even in the car yet and they were squabbling again.

"Come on girls," he pleaded. "There's not time for this. Please. I've got enough trouble with your mother. She's packed half the house, left me to get it into the car, and now she's in the shower, singing! If we miss that ferry, we won't get on another – not at this time of the year. They're all full." He tried to open the front door without dropping everything, but fumbled with the latch, tripped over and banged his nose on the doormat.

The girls' quarrel was forgotten as they dashed down to pick him up, muffling their giggles with sympathetic noises.

***

Half an hour later the car turned onto the main road.

Charlie was wearing her jodhpurs.

"How was I to know you'd left them out specially?" said Mum." I thought they looked dirty so I put them in the wash-basket."

"There you are. I told you they were smelly." Rosie smirked at her little sister. She put out her tongue and waggled it at Charlie who retaliated by giving Rosie a pinch on the nearest arm.

Dad turned his head sharply and glared at them. "If either of you mentions those blessed jodhpurs again," he said, "there'll be no Ireland. Do I make myself clear? You sound like a couple of five year-olds. Grow up, the pair of you." He pulled masterfully into the outside lane, saw a large van bearing down on him and hastily retreated.

"Why you want to travel in them, I don't know," said Mum as she shuffled through all the tickets and bits of paper Dad had given her to hold.

The hotel looked lovely on the website, and it was a really good family deal, and they'd all agreed that it was a real bonus that the girls would be able to ride out there. Even so, Mum sighed. "Seems to me you're never out or riding clothes, you girls. Did you bring any skirts or dresses, Rosie? Or is that a silly question?"

Rosie shared a pony that belonged to her friend Nicola. She was away at school and wanted someone to exercise him. He was in livery a short bike ride away, and Rosie's bike was never at home these days. Mum didn't ride herself, and although she liked horses well enough, she'd never sat on one, and really didn't want to spend her life with them! She sometimes wondered if Rosie might begin to grow out of ponies soon, but Charlie was a different matter.

Charlie might even go on to work with horses, make them her job, and her passion.

She spent all her free time mucking out and helping at the riding school and was allowed to ride other people's ponies in exchange, but Mum knew that she wanted her own pony more than anything in the world. She was only ten, nearly three years younger than her sister, but she was fearless, and even Rosie said she was the better rider. She said it reluctantly, and when her sister wasn't around, but she said it.

"I haven't got a dress, "Charlie announced proudly. "I like jodhpurs or jeans. Dresses are for sissies."

"Will we have to change out of our riding things for meals and stuff at the hotel?" Rosie asked anxiously, "I hope it won't be smart. What do you think, Dad?"

"I think you should be grateful that we're taking you on holiday at all" he replied. "I sometimes wonder why I bother doing anything with you two. All you do is squabble or moan."

Mum patted his hand soothingly, and turned to the girls. "Don't take any notice. He loves you really. Car travel always brings out the worst in him. Doesn't it, dear?"

***

The iron-grey pony with white spots on his back stood pressed against the wall of the stable. He was a Connemara, pure bred, though to look at him now you wouldn't have known. He was painfully thin and very nervous. The other pony was bigger than him and solidly built, and didn't like an intruder in his stable.

There was a rusty-looking tin in the corner with some water in it. The grey pony didn't try to drink, although he'd had no water all day and it was hot and stuffy in this stable. He'd gone towards the tin when he first came in here and the other pony had barged him against the door and kicked him. His hock was already swelling, and it hurt. He was scared and confused, but this wasn't a new feeling for him. It had been with him most of his short life.

Born late in the year, he'd always been bullied by the other foals, and when it had been time to wean them from their mothers he'd suffered more than most. She had sensed that he really needed her still, and had called continually to him. When the stud people moved her further away from him, she called even more frantically, and this made him struggle through the fence to reach her. He broke a post, then tore his leg on it. The wound was deep and he lost a lot of blood before he was found.

After four weeks of being kept in a stable to rest, his leg healed and he went out again, but the bullying continued, and the new year found him a sad and weedy yearling. He was a poor prospect for the stud profit-wise, so one of the grooms bought him cheap and took him home. He picked up a little as the spring grass came through, and he enjoyed the attention from the children there. But they had no stable and not much money to spare, so at the end of the summer the groom sold him on to some tinkers he knew.

The spotted pony spent his first working days trotting along behind a cart, or standing tethered at the roadside surrounded by dogs and children. They weren't unkind but they were rather rough with him. They broke him to ride in a headcollar, but he was still thin and found it hard to keep up with the carts for more than an hour or two at a time. Late in the summer as the tinkers approached Galway and set up camp at their usual place, they were glad to see a dealer they knew from Connemara drive onto the site. He often bought horses from them, and he always said, "A pure Connie is a gift from heaven, as easy to sell as a pint of good Guinness."

He cast his eye over the handful of horses tethered around the vans, and gladly accepted the nip of Irish the tinker's wife offered him. One eyebrow went up as he got to the grey gelding.

"Well now, this one is not a great example of the breed, I must say. What age is he? "The tinker scratched his chin. "He's two now," he said, "and he's just starting to grow. You've caught him at an in-between stage. Didn't he look just great about two weeks ago?"

His eldest son nodded in agreement, and popped his baby brother up onto the pony's back. The pony didn't bother to raise his head from the grass and the boy said triumphantly, "There now, look at that! He'll make a lovely riding pony, sir!" The pony moved forward in search of better grass and the boy whipped the toddler off again and put him on the ground. The child threw back his head and began to bawl and the dealer moved hastily out of earshot. "Have you his papers?" He asked suspiciously. "Are you sure now that he's pure-bred?" He wasn't going to pay much for a 'dog' like that. The tinker dug in the pocket of his huge coat, and produced a sheaf of greasy papers. He spat on his fingers and pulled out the breed registration certificate for the spotted pony.

"He is as kind as a Christian, sir," he assured the dealer. "Sure, doesn't little Maureen ride him on her own, and her not four yet?"

The dealer seemed to remember that little Maureen was "not four yet" last year either, but decided to let that pass. The pony was very quiet, with a kind manner, and he got him very cheap in the end.

* * *

This dealer was a hard-drinking, gambling man and one night in his cups he lost a good deal of money at cards to a man who ran a bar near the seaside. As the cards he was dealt got worse and the debt continued to grow, the dealer started to think of a way out.

"Well now Seamus," he said, looking at a spot just above the other man's head, "I've an idea. You've got yourself a trekking place I hear. So I'll make you an offer. Let's cut the pack, one card each, highest card wins. If I win, you let me off what I owe ya. If you win, you can have this lovely grey pony I bought a while ago. He's been running with my boys on the farm, but I've no rider for him, now the kids have gone and left their poor old father to make the best of things in his own. God bless them! Scattered all over the world they are now! And do they write to me? They do not. Ah well! Now what was I saying? Oh yes – the pony. Pure-bred Connie he is. A lovely looker. He's just what you need for those posh foreign customers of yours. He's as gentle as a lamb, and as strong as an ox. Seamus, you'll love him! Now, will you cut the cards first or shall I?"

When Seamus Keenan sobered up next day and went to collect his winnings, his face fell.

"Strong as an ox?" he grumbled. "Did he say strong as an ox?" He looked at the pony in disbelief. 'Weak as a kitten' or 'timid as a mouse', were the phrases he would have used. And it had obviously never seen a trailer before. It was lucky that he was a burly man. He had to use all his weight to get it in. It was a lousy journey back to the yard, and when he put the pony into the box with Jacko, it slunk into the corner and stood there, shivering. "Huh, 'strong as an ox'?" he muttered to himself. "Damn dealers. Damn cards. Well, that's the last time," he muttered. "From now on, when I play, it's cash on the table!" He slammed the door of his red van, revved up the engine and drove furiously out of the yard.

A teenage boy with black hair and blue eyes came out of the tackroom. He'd ducked in there when he heard his father's van, knowing he'd have a real bad head and a temper to match this morning. He looked over the door at the new arrival, slid back the bolt, and went in. Jacko put his ears back.

"Don't you dare you old devil," the boy said. Then he reached out a hand to the new grey pony, who flinched and pulled back, his eyes rolling in fear. "Now, now, come on little man. I'm going to see that nobody hurts you anymore. At least I'm going to try," he added ruefully. He was guessing that this pony had had a tough time, and he was still only a baby. He'd a nice frame, but was so skinny and backward. Would life be much better for him here?

"I'll do my best," he whispered. "What shall we call you eh, little man?" He stroked his nose. "What about Micky, that suit ya?" He was about to move Jacko aside so the pony could drink, when an angry voice stopped him.

"Are you going to stand there messin' with that thing all morning?" Fiona, the girl in charge, had just walked in to the yard. "We've got four riders coming in five minutes and I want them ponies tacked up and ready to go. Time's money you know, and yer da wouldn't like to hear you've been mooning about over that hopeless creature. He'll be no use to us. We've not got enough ponies fit at the moment, and that'll not be up to carrying much weight by the look of it."

"And did you see your da's face? He knows old Carmody's taken him for a ride!" As Tom got on with his work, he vowed he'd do everything in his power to help the new pony.

* * *

"I thought we came on holiday to enjoy ourselves." Dad looked down at his two daughters.

He was fed up.

He might have known.

They'd only been in Connemara one day. His heart had sunk when they arrived last night and saw the dilapidated state of the stables at the bottom of the hotel garden.

'Just my luck!' he'd thought. If it had only been Charlie who was worried, he wouldn't have taken much notice. In spite of wearing boys' clothes and having no interest in anything feminine, she was a real softy at heart, and like a soggy marshmallow when it came to animals. But now Rosie, normally so sensible and grown up, seemed, if anything, more concerned than her sister.

"How can we Dad?" she said. "How can we enjoy stuff, knowing that he's stuck in that place with no sign of food or water? There's no room to move and the other horses have been biting and kicking him, and he's so thin."

"OK," he sighed. "Go and book a ride. Then you can check up properly on how they're all kept. I hope you're not exaggerating this. And then, can we please go out somewhere in the car and have a look at this beautiful country? You can see all the horses you want, back home."

When they'd booked a week at this hotel, they all sat down together and read the brochure. '*Trek across the glorious wild countryside on our pure-bred Connemara ponies*' it had said. Unfortunately they'd now discovered it was a rather old brochure, and the hotel had a new owner who was extremely keen on golf.

The girls went to the reception desk and asked about the riding.

"Ah well now, that's nothing to do with us anymore," the woman said, putting down her teacup and smiling." You'll have to ask at the yard. See Fiona. She's in charge, or Tom, or Sean. Their father's the new owner. Oh it's a beautiful day for a ride, so enjoy yourselves."

Everyone was so friendly here, and the sun came out as they crossed the lawn and went through the gate to the stable yard. Rosie even thought, 'Maybe we're being silly. Maybe things seemed so bad last night was because we were tired, and it was late.

But no, the yard was still dirty, with bits of rusty machinery all over the place. The ponies were still two to a box, and the floors were filthy. There was no water in some of the stables. The ponies' feet were still uncared for – and the spotted grey one was still painfully thin.

A door stood open and on the floor they could see an assortment of tack, none of it very clean, and some of it cracked and broken. A boy came out of the tackroom. He was very good-looking with black hair and bright blue eyes, but he was in a bad mood.

"Yes – what are you two after?" he said. "The stables are closed 'til this afternoon, if you want a ride" – he looked at their jodhpurs and shining boots – "which I suppose ya do. Put your names on that list. Me brother Tom'll be back at two, and he'll be goin' out at two thirty and again at four thirty, so suit yourselves. I don't take the rides."

He brought a cigarette from behind his back and as he walked off he blew a smoke ring past the battered sign that said, NO SMOKING, BEWARE OF FIRES.

The girls stared after him.

Rosie said, "I bet this place was OK before these new people took over. It's all properly laid out, and there are racks for the saddles and bridles in there, why don't they use them?"

Charlie didn't answer. She was hanging over the door and looking at the grey pony. "He's a Connemara all right. Look at his lovely head, but he's so thin and even more nervous than he was last night. This other one's not so bad. Poor grey boy's really scared of him. If you ride that one, I'll try and get on grey boy and see if I can get him to relax a bit."

'Yes,' thought Rosie grudgingly, 'and you probably will.' She couldn't find the list the boy had mentioned, so she wrote on a scrap of paper: "Please can two girls ride at 2:30 today? Thank you. R. Jackson."

They stuck it in a crack of the door and went back for lunch with Mum and Dad.

Dad asked, rather plaintively, if after the ride they could all go for a swim in the sea. He said they must spend some time away from horses!

They were back in the yard by 2 o'clock sharp and were

surprised to see the black-haired boy wearing a battered riding hat and getting some ponies ready. He seemed gentle with a little bay mare as he led her out, and when Charlie said, "I thought you didn't take the rides?" they were both startled to hear a rather different voice reply.

"Who told you that? Now – can you both ride?" He looked at them suspiciously.

The girls were dressed for the job, but then many of his customers were, and it soon became obvious that the riding clothes had only just come out of their wrappers, and the wearers didn't know one end of a horse from the other.

Rosie and Charlie didn't answer, but the look on their faces told him they were a little offended, so he went on hastily: "We'll take Magic and Pimpernel and Johnny, the three bays here..."

"Oh no, please," Charlie jumped up and down excitedly, "please could I ride this grey, Grey Boy...please. I must!"

Tom opened his mouth to say, "Micky? Oh no, he's not up to it," but, as he looked at her determined face, he heard himself say instead, "Well, OK, but if we take him, we'll not go far in this heat. He's still quite new here and not settled in too well yet..."

"Anyone can see that!" Charlie interrupted him. She was about to go on, but her sister moved quickly between them.

"Charlie, don't be rude!" she exclaimed, and delivered a swift little kick on the shin. Charlie squeaked in pain and hopped about, glaring.

"Please excuse her. She thinks she's the only one who knows anything about horses. We ride quite a lot, at home in England. I'm Rosie, by the way and this is my sister Charlotte."

At the use of her hated full name, Charlie glared even more fiercely at Rosie who continued firmly, "I share a pony with a friend, so we do know a bit about them...and we think..." She hesitated. It was too soon to say anything. It might not be his fault... Best to ride first and try and find out more about this place, the people who owned it and about the grey spotted pony.

* * *

Rosie rode Magic, and Tom was on Pimpernel. Johnny went back in his box, and Micky came thankfully out. Between them they found a saddle that fitted reasonably well, but the bridle was awful, with a harsh straight-bar bit, more like a driving bit. The reins didn't even match and they were cracked and dry. "Don't you ever clean the tack?" asked Charlie. Tom flushed, and Rosie quickly said, "We could give you a hand if you like, we're here for a week." He smiled at her. They were certainly different from the usual people who came for a 'pony ride'.

He noticed that Charlie looked quite at home on Micky's back. He threw his head and skittered about, but she dropped her hands and sat completely still until he began to calm down. Before they were even out of sight of the stables, Micky seemed to unclench his teeth and relax a little.

The girls didn't want a fast ride. That made a change. Most guests wanted what they thought was at least one good gallop. These girls were much more keen to talk, and as they went quietly round the fields they plied Tom with questions.

He realised they'd mistaken him for Sean, and when Charlie said in her blunt way: "Don't you want to smoke now?" he laughed and said. "I do not!! It'll be Sean you met this morning. I've got a twin brother. We've both blue shirts on today. I don't smoke. He's the one with all the vices, and he hates horses really, except to bet on them. He thinks Dad's mad to bother with these. He only likes racehorses. Thinks these lot are 'dogs'."

"Well I love dogs," said Charlie, and they laughed.

"Have you always ridden?" Rosie asked him, after they'd walked in silence for a while. "I have, I can't remember a time when I didn't. I'd like to get into racing one day, be a jockey, a great jockey. Ride a horse like Desert Orchid, or even Arkle."

His blue eyes were wistful as he trotted a little way ahead.

Rosie didn't know who Arkle was. She decided to ask Dad as soon as possible. Charlie had stayed behind with Micky, and now as she caught up with her sister, she had a serious look on her face.

"Rosie, I need this pony," she whispered. "I mean it. I can feel that he trusts me! I think he's been waiting for me to find him." She leant forward and gently stroked his thin neck.

"Oh don't be so ridiculous!" Rosie retorted. "We don't know anything about him, that's just silly talk!" Although as she said it, a bit of her thought – 'but I do wish we could help him, poor thing…'

As they turned for home, Tom said, "I've not seen Micky look so happy since he got here. He definitely likes you. I don't know what sort of a life he's had 'til now. Dad won him in a poker game. It's the devil of a game, isn't it, poker!"

Both girls looked blankly at him. Maybe the English didn't play cards for money.

Tom wished his dad didn't. Sean did sometimes too and this worried Tom.

His dad owned a bar with a big kids' playground and an amusement arcade, and it was full all summer, but there never seemed to be any spare money. Often in the winter there didn't seem to be any money at all. He supposed that was why his mum had gone. She left five years ago. His dad used to shout at her all the time and they fought a lot, but how Tom missed her! He sometimes had a lovely dream that she'd come back, and then woke up feeling awful and lonely. This girl Rosie reminded him of her in some ways. So quiet, and yet she seemed strong and kind.

"What am I thinking about?" he said to himself, "I only met them half an hour ago! Pull yourself together Tom Keenan, you're going soft!"

When they got back to the yard, Rosie deliberately put Micky in with Magic and filled up their water can. Tom watched her do it and said nothing. Magic had a drink, then turned her back on Micky, rested a foot and promptly went to sleep. Charlie put her arms around Micky's neck and whispered, "I'll be back."

And she was.

* * *

Except for a drive to the nearest town, for saddle soap, fly repellent and some wound powder, she and Rosie spent all their time there for the next two days. Dad and Mum gave up trying to organise any other outings with them.

"Well, at least it means we have a few days to ourselves," Mum said.

Dad grinned, thinking that, yes, perhaps they could have a bit of fun without the girls in tow. "All right your Ladyship, maybe you could drive today? And...maybe...we could try out one or two of those cosy-looking bars we keep passing." He grinned again, and Mum laughed and led the way to the car.

The only fly in the ointment was Fiona, the girl who ran the stables. She resented the girls interfering, and gave Tom a hard time about his friendship with "them stuck-up-nose-in-the-air-know-it-all English busybodies!"

Luckily Fiona had a lot of riders who wanted to go out for the whole day along the coast, so the girls were able to sit and clean the tack and even mend some of the broken pieces.

Charlie found an old snaffle bit and put it onto Micky's bridle. She hid the sharp-edged one in the middle of the muck heap. She'd looked closely at Micky's face and it was a mass of scars, from bites and cuts. She doused him in wound powder, after washing them all in salt water. He let her do this, but only if she kept her movements very gentle and slow.

As he was so thin, she didn't really want to keep riding him. Instead she led him out when Fiona wasn't there and let him graze on any decent grass they could find.

Rosie and Tom cleaned out all the boxes, and tied up some of the fencing. They also cleared the droppings in the field. That took them ages, as it obviously had not been done for a very long time. Tom told Rosie he'd tried to get more grazing for them all, but that his dad couldn't pay for it. He didn't say he *wouldn't* pay, but Rosie guessed that was the truth of it.

She really liked Tom and now could hardly believe she'd ever confused him with Sean. They'd seen Sean drinking in the bar they'd all gone to last night. The girl at the hotel had told Dad about Tom's mum leaving, so Rosie knew his life was not easy. They were re-fastening the wire on a fence by the yard entrance – and she was holding the hammer for him. As she looked at his scruffy shirt, and the pocket falling off his jeans, she found herself thinking she'd like to look after him. He turned and grinned at her over the fence wire and she blushed scarlet. When he smiled at her she felt very odd. As she handed him the hammer, their hands touched for an instant, and then they both nearly jumped out of their skins when a voice behind them roared.

"Well, well, now this is cosy. Getting on nicely together aren't we? May I ask you Tom Keenan what you think you're doing? Getting the guests to do all the work! Do you want to get us all thrown off the hotel land? What do you think would happen to your precious ponies then eh? eh? It's a good job I've got Fiona to rely on. She knows what's what. And she told me you were messing about."

Rosie looked at the man. Tom's dad wasn't very tall, but he

was big: big in every way – big head, big shoulders, big stomach and big voice. He smirked at Rosie, and she felt all horrid inside, as if he'd found out something secret about her.

"Well now Tom, why aren't ya off out with the other guests? You're supposed to be so charming, go off and charm some more cash out of their pockets and into mine."

He ignored Rosie now and advanced on his son, only to stop and look over his shoulder as Charlie appeared, leading Micky quietly back into the yard. "What's this? Why isn't that tinker's pony working?"

Micky's ears went back at the sound of his voice. "I'm not buying feed for ponies that don't pull their weight. If he doesn't work he's going!" Micky pulled back as if to get away from the man, and before Rosie could warn her to keep quiet, Charlie retorted: "Feed! This pony doesn't look as if he's had a proper feed in his life. He's as thin as a rake. And look at his feet. All his heels are cracked, and this front one's badly bruised. And when did you last worm any of these ponies? You ought to be ashamed of yourself. He needs a vet and a farrier."

The big man stared down at her, his mouth open. He couldn't seem to think of anything to say. Obviously nobody had ever spoken to him like that before. And certainly not a child! He wobbled slightly as he turned and pushed past Tom, and Rosie suddenly realised he must have been drinking. Poor Tom, no wonder his mum had run away. And Sean looked like following in his father's ways. Poor Tom...

And poor Micky. Charlie tried to calm him but the sight of Seamus Keenan had obviously upset him. Rosie wondered again what else might have happened to him, and as if Tom read her mind, he said: "Micky's scared of men, I'm afraid he's had a hard life before we got him. And he's such a baby. This life doesn't suit him and it never will. He needs a loving owner, who'll bring him on quietly. And let him grow into himself. Then he'd make someone a grand pony. No, poor Micky this life could be the death of him." He took the lead rope from Charlie and put Micky into the box with Magic. "I had to move him again today," he went on angrily. "Fiona had him back in with Jacko. No wonder he's covered in bites." His fingers touched an gash on the pony's neck just under the mane. "Right!" said Rosie. "Put green gel on the list. We'll send Dad shopping again."

"You mustn't spend your money," Tom protested.

Charlie butted in, "I'd spend all of mine to look after him if he was *my* pony."

"Your pony," said Tom, "if only he was your pony... If only you could..."

Charlie stopped in her tracks, then looked at Tom with growing excitement in her eyes. "If only we could what?" she gasped.

Rosie turned towards her, remembering what she'd said the first time she'd sat on Mickey.

Charlie ran over to the door of his box. "I need this pony!" She announced to Tom. "So I'm not going to say 'if only'!" Rosie tried to interrupt her, but Charlie just went on "All right Rosie, I know what you're thinking, but at least I'm saying...*maybe*! Maybe we could take him with us...maybe he could live at the stables...maybe nice people could ride him...I'll save all my money...I'll make him my pony...because I *need* him and he *needs* me!"

Rosie looked at her sister, and thought of Dad's face, and she sighed.

Tom heard her sigh, and came back down to earth with a bump. "There's just the little problem of your mother and father," said Tom, "And how would you get him back to England?" He sighed. 'And how much would my father want for him?' he thought to himself. The pony had cost his dad nothing, but Tom knew he'd take every penny he could squeeze out of them. He suspected that the girls weren't all that well off, otherwise they'd both have had their own ponies by now, the keenness of them. He saw their faces drop a little and used that as an excuse to put an arm round each girl's shoulder.

"What we need now is a plan of campaign," he said. "We must mobilise all our forces, and work out what's best to be done, and the first thing we must do is...to tell your parents that *they* need this pony."

The girls laughed.

Rosie looked up into Tom's face and suddenly felt that almost anything was possible.

***

"We need what?" exclaimed Dad. "I wondered why you two had suddenly got keen on bird watching. You crafty pair, you must think I came down with the last shower of rain."

He put down his binoculars and lay back on the sand.

Mum was rummaging in her beach bag for her sunglasses.

"Don't be silly, Rosie," she said. "We couldn't possibly afford to buy him and take him all the way home. Now Charlie," she held up her hand, "we know you're desperate for a pony of your own, but this is just nonsensical. Out of the question."

"Oh he's got one," shouted Dad.

Charlie gazed miserably at the cormorant flashing by with the fish glinting in its beak. If only she could scoop up Micky so easily.

Rosie was persisting, "If we could organise some cheap transport," she said. "Mum, if we leave him here...I'm really worried about him. He won't survive."

"Of course he'll survive! Things can't be that bad." Mum lay down on her towel again. "We can't take him back with us, and that's final."

"Then I'm staying here," said Charlie, and set off back up the beach at a run.

"You could have all my premium bonds, Dad," Rosie said, "and hers." She looked at her sister's fast-disappearing back. "He's got lovely paces and I'm sure he'll jump one day. He'll be worth something once he's sorted out. You'd get your money back in the end."

Dad gave up and put the binoculars back into their case.

"Rosie this is ridiculous. I'm going to have some lunch and then I'm going to have a siesta. We're here for a holiday, to rest and have a good time, and I'm not letting you two ruin it all with fantasies about ponies. Do I make myself clear?"

"Now look what you've done." Mum grumbled as she hauled herself off the sand and gathered up her beach things. "It's about time you girls started to consider other people, and stopped thinking about yourselves." She stumped off after her husband, leaving Rosie sitting alone.

As she gazed out to sea, she said to herself: "But we are thinking of others. We're thinking of Micky. And Tom says he'll die if we can't take him home!" A single tear rolled down her nose and landed on the sand in front of her.

***

While Rosie was wandering along the beach in search of her sister, Tom was in trouble at the yard. Sean was still out somewhere, celebrating their twin birthday and Fiona was late. This was very unusual for her. She took a great pride in being seen to be efficient. This meant always turning up in good time, looking smart and tidy, and always saying all the right things to the customers. (Unfortunately for the horses that's as far as it went and her 'efficiency' did not include proper care for their welfare.) Tom was trying to pacify five people who were waiting for a ride. They had driven over from Dublin yesterday to '*feel the genuine atmosphere of the West Coast, and to ride a real Connemara pony on the windswept beach*' – as promised by the out-of-date brochure – and they only had an hour before they had to leave. They were catching a plane to London for a glimpse of 'Vieille Angleterre' before going home to Paris at the weekend.

Tom dashed into the tackroom and grabbed a saddle for Johnny.

'What a way to spend me birthday,' he thought, 'running round after this one and her brood.'

The thin woman looked at her watch again and sighed: "We want to go to ze craft shop before it close," she said crossly, "then we 'av to catch a plane from Shannon. Zis time is not good. Maybe we don't wait."

Her foot was tapping impatiently on the newly polished floor of the tackroom.

A fat boy slapped his leg with an obviously new hunting crop. A sister sighed and gestured at him to stop, so he slapped her leg instead, and a fracas ensued. The mother grabbed one child in each hand and shouted at Tom: "OK, enough. We go – no riding – OK?"

Tom knew his father would be very angry at the loss of five paying customers and breathed a sigh of relief when Fiona's old car came creaking round the corner, just as the French family reached it.

It was full of people. Fiona was driving, and two American girls, who must have been at least twenty, were in the back with Sean squeezed in between them. Their cheeks were flushed, and Tom guessed they'd been to a birthday gathering at his father's bar.

Fiona got out and spoke to the waiting woman.

"Oh dear me. I'm so sorry, Mrs Chollet, or should I say Madame?" she smiled ingratiatingly at her. "My car has been playing up all this week. Now then, let's get everyone on. Your horses are all ready. Tom should have got you all mounted. I don't know what he was thinking of! My, my, you look smart." She lifted one small girl onto Johnny's hairy back and shortened the stirrups for her.

Then she turned and glared at Tom. "Get the other brats on," she muttered under her breath. "And be quick about it."

She turned to the Frenchwoman again, saying, "I think you'll like this mare. She's half-sister to a National winner, Madame. She has a real touch of class. Wait one moment and I'll give you a leg up, then we'll be off in a jiffy."

Tom watched them all clatter off up the lane. He wondered

how much the woman understood, and whether she was taken in by the load of rubbish Fiona was giving her. Then his thoughts were interrupted by his brother's voice. Sean was still in the back of the car with the two girls, and now they clambered out, laughing.

"Sure you can ride too, girls," Sean was saying. "We'll all go out, now, together. We'll soon catch up with the others, so we will. Then I'll show you my secret caves along by the sea here. Tom'll get them ready for us, won't you Tommy Tiddler?"

"We've not enough ponies," Tom said firmly. "Magic's on three legs, Jacko kicked her."

"Aw, never mind the trekking. We'd really like to do some jumping," one of the girls said. "Could you fix that, Seany babe?"

'Seany babe' slapped the blond one on the backside.

"Indeed I could, my lady." He bowed deeply. "Your wish is my command."

They giggled.

"OI'll give youse both a lesson," he drawled in an exaggerated Irish accent, and they giggled again.

"Hey that'd be just great," the dark one said. "You Irish are such fabulous riders. Hey do you know Eddie Macken? Does he live round here?"

"That old boy? Know him? I do indeed," said Sean. "In fact, he taught me all I know about horses."

Tom turned away. He was ashamed of his brother.

"Get them two out," Sean shouted at him. "I'll fix the jumps out the back."

"There's only Jacko left," Tom said. "I told you, Magic can't put her foot to the ground."

The girls followed Tom's look and stared into the stable at Magic.

"Oh gee, just look at her! Oh, poor baby. Is the vet on his way?"

"He is, he is," Sean assured them. "Tom's waiting for the vet now, don't you worry."

Tom couldn't believe his brother could tell so many lies in such a short time. The bolder of the two girls caught hold of Sean's arm.

"Hey! Who's this cute little grey one with the spots?" she asked, pulling at his sleeve and wrinkling her nose. "Can I ride him?"

Tom hastily got between her and Micky's door. "He's not being ridden just now, he's not up to it. He's new here and…"

"You can. You can, you can ride anything you like, me darlin'." Sean beamed at the dark-haired American, then hissed at his brother. "Da said this morning that if this little rat doesn't work, he'll be off to the knacker. So make up your mind, if she doesn't ride him now, I'll tell Da, then he'll be off you know where! Nice birthday present for ya, eh?"

Tom stepped back. He felt helpless. He could only pray that Charlie and Rosie didn't appear for the next half hour or so.

At least the girl was slim and quite small, and she wasn't rough when she got on and asked Micky to move. The pony had begun to sweat a little though. Micky didn't like Sean anymore than he liked his father – the man who'd beaten him up to get him into the trailer and bring him here.

"Well now Tommy Tiddler – bro – your precious Micky. Micky Mouse I call him." Sean grinned at the Americans. "Because he's afraid of his own shadow. Let's see what he can do."

Tom stood in misery as the other girl mounted Jacko. He watched Sean break a long whippy stick out of the hedge and walk through the gateway. There was a piece of rough ground at the side of the hotel's new extension, and it was on to this that Sean led the ponies. Two makeshift jumps – just old wings that didn't match and bits of poles – were standing out in the Connemara sunshine. The ground was rough, rutted and stony. You wouldn't want to do any flatwork on it, let alone jump. "Sean, you must let them stretch their legs first," Tom called. "They've been standing in for the last two hours."

Sean ignored him, and walked over to the blonde girl on

Jacko. "Turn around and come over this one, come towards me, darlin'."

The first pole was about seventy-five centimetres off the ground – no ground line – nothing, but Jacko knew better than to stop. In spite of stumbling on the rough surface he cleared the pole quite easily, then went round and jumped it again.

The other girl then followed, but when they got to the pole Micky stopped. Tom was watching from a distance. He realised the pony had no idea what he was supposed to do. Sean wasn't going to let a pony behave like that.

"Bring 'im round again, don't let him get away with that," Sean shouted. "Get a hold of his head darlin'. Make him do what you want."

The girl gathered up the reins and kicked the pony on. But the same thing happened again, only this time Micky ducked out to the side at the sight of Sean waving the stick at him. He tried to run across the grass to get away, but was confronted with the other jump. This one had a tatty old gate swinging on the cups. He banged into it and knocked it off. The clatter frightened him. He started to panic, swung round and the girl came off sideways, luckily landing on her feet. When Sean ran up and grabbed the reins, Micky's neck was bathed in sweat.

Tom dashed over. "Don't hit him! He doesn't know what you want him to do."

"Happy birthday to you. Happy birthday Mr Knackerman," Sean crooned viciously at Tom. "Now you stay there me darlin'," he shouted to the girl. "He's a bit green this one. I'll sort him out."

He vaulted on, landing with a thump on Micky's bony back. He crossed the stirrups in front of the saddle, to show how little he needed them, and he brought the stick down three or four times on Micky's rump. Tom, unable to bear it, was about to dash forward again when he caught sight of a movement in one of the hotel windows, and he stopped in his tracks. Rosie and Charlie's mum and dad – just up from their siesta – were staring down at the scene below them. Tom moved back and looked away in case his brother should notice them up there...

Sean managed to beat Micky over the pole eventually, and then got the girls to raise it up to about a metre. Micky was terrified now, bewildered, and in pain from the blows to his head as well as to his back. Sean seemed to have forgotten the people around him in his desire to dominate the pony, and the American girls were finding the handsome Irish boy less appealing with every stroke of the stick. In desperation Tom ran forward and tried to pull it out of Sean's hand, only to receive a stinging blow across his arm.

Suddenly the window was flung open and a voice shouted: "Stop that this minute, do you hear? I'm going straight to the hotel manager and he'll report you! Leave that poor animal alone. Don't you hit him again. Your father's going hear about this, you…you hooligan." Dad was scarlet in the face, and Mum beside him was as white as a sheet.

The American girls now turned on Sean too.

"How awful, we've never seen anyone treating a horse like that. You Irish are supposed to be so kind. We're going back to the hotel" They beat a hasty retreat and the sound of their voices trailed off as they disappeared, "I'd no idea he was so awful. And he was drunk! What a stupid, awful kid."

Suddenly brave, Tom shouted up at his twin. "Awful kid? Selfish spoilt brat is more like it. And a bully too. Look at this poor little horse."

Sean hurled himself off Micky's back, and the brothers rolled together on the ground. "You're the one who's spoilt." Sean ground out the words, his fists flailing at his brother. "Always Mummy's pet! She always liked you best. I don't know why, you puny, animal-loving softy. Why did she always take your side eh, *and* she writes to you. I know, I seen the envelopes. I seen you reading them, and hiding them when Da comes by. Sixteen today? You're more like six. You're not a man, you're just a silly babyish mummy's boy without your mummy to look after you anymore."

Tom didn't know where he got the strength from, but his fist shot out and Sean was suddenly flat on his back in some brambles. He lay there winded. His eye was already starting to close and there was a bright red mark on his cheek. He started to get up to retaliate, and then saw Rosie and Charlie's dad, still standing at the open window. Dad's face was like thunder, and he raised a finger in a gesture of warning.

Gradually Sean seemed to shrink, until he was like a small boy again. He stumbled back into the yard, resisting the temptation to lash out at Micky, who was standing, trembling and exhausted, near the gate. When Tom looked up at the hotel window, Mum and Dad had gone. He gathered up the two ponies, put them away gently removing Micky's tack and talking quietly to him. Then he went to wash his hands and face at the yard tap.

Sean had taken Tom's bike and bundled out and away down the road to the village. Tom was so glad to see the back of him he didn't even think about the prospect of the three-mile walk home for his tea.

As it turned out he didn't walk anywhere. Rosie and Charlie had got wind of his birthday. They arrived at the stables just as the French family were departing, and an hour later, Tom and the girls were sitting in the hotel garden with Mum and Dad. They all sang as Tom pushed a knife into a delicious chocolate sponge with SIXTEEN TODAY, HAPPY BIRTHDAY TOM written on it in pink and blue icing.

"The hotel chef's done us proud," said Mum and they all agreed it was delicious as they had a second slice.

"Now then, girls...and Tom." said Dad. "Your attention please. I've got an announcement to make. Your mum and I have been talking, girls...and Tom," he added again, and Rosie flushed with pleasure at the expression on Tom's face. "Yes. Well now, I think you may all have guessed by now? We've been talking and maybe this idea of yours about Micky is not quite so mad after all."

Charlie and Rosie stopped chewing cake simultaneously, and Tom nearly choked on his piece.

"You mean...?" he stammered." You mean...you would be able to take him over to England...and look after him...give him a home?"

The other guests never quite knew where all the flying bits of cake came from.

They just saw three youngsters leaping and hugging each other and dancing round in circles between the tables on the lawn. Really, young people nowadays! Still, everybody knew the Irish were all quite mad.

***

While Tom Keenan was dancing on the lawn, Sean Keenan was trudging along the road scowling. As he'd cycled away from the stables, the Guinness had suddenly got hold of him and he'd wobbled off the road and into a bush, so now he was limping as well as nursing a black eye, and his temper was getting worse. Trust his brother's bike to hurl him off. He hated his brother...trying to tell him what to do...and that damned grey pony! Useless little rat it was anyway. Oh, he hated Tom all right and he was goin' to fix him now. Give him a sixteenth birthday to remember.

***

Mum, Dad, the two girls and Tom walked into Keenan's bar at about six o'clock that night. Tom and the girls had bathed the wheals on Micky's neck and they'd left him an hour ago in his stable on his own. He seemed to be OK, though his legs had swollen up a bit and he was walking rather carefully. Although the horses were usually turned out into the field at night, they'd left Magic in the next door box for company, and they both had a fresh pile of hay that Dad had gone to the farmer's store – again – to buy. The first excitement had died down and they had talked seriously about how they could possibly get Micky home. Luckily Tom had a friend whose uncle moved horses about for a living – "Only in a small way, just one small horse box, a blue one," Tom said. "But he does go to England quite often" – and the friend had been asked to find out when the next trip might be.

"I'm not leaving until Micky does," Charlie announced.

"Yes, well, we'll see about that," said Mum. "And anyway let's not make any plans 'til everything is settled. Many a slip before the chickens are hatched. Or is it many a mickle makes a muckle?"

"Whatever you're trying to say," said Dad, laughing in spite of himself. "I think our minds are now made up. We're going to try and take the pony away from here. There's just the question of the money."

Tom's heart sank a little. Seamus Keenan wouldn't make it easy, or cheap, for them. Tom was sure of that.

To their surprise, instead of Seamus, they found Fiona behind the bar, grumpily waiting for the Guinness to settle as she served a group of locals. Sean was slumped in a corner, a bag of crisps and an empty glass in front of him. When he heard his brother's voice he looked up and laughed. It wasn't a nice laugh, Rosie thought, and what had happened to his eye? (Mum and Dad hadn't told the girls everything that had happened outside their hotel window that afternoon.)

"We'd like to speak to Mr Keenan," Dad said.

"Would ya now?" said Fiona. "Well he'll not be back for an hour or so. He's away to the knacker with that pathetic pony. When he saw what it had done to Sean's face, kicking him like that, and then it had half-killed one of the guests, throwing her off on her head, well that settled it. He'll be there by now I dare say, Mr Phelan never closes, not if there's a bit of money to be made."

She turned away and handed a foaming glass to a little man with shiny black eyes.

"Good health to youse all," he said to Tom and his friends, as he raised the Guinness to his lips.

They turned as one and dashed for the door,

"Oh well," the little man muttered. "That's the English for ya, always rushing here there and everywhere, well good luck to them," and he drained his glass in one go.

* * *

They drove straight back to the stables, and as Charlie and Rosie leapt from the car they could all hear Magic calling.

"Oh no," cried Tom. "He's already gone."

And sure enough the door to Micky's box was swinging in the wind, the hay half-eaten on the floor, and Magic, distressed at being left on her own, was tossing her head and spinning around in her box. Mum was waving her mobile: "What's this man's number, Tom? Quick!" Tom grabbed a grubby phone list from the notice board, and while Dad reversed the car, Rosie picked up a headcollar and dashed Magic through the field gate. The mare trotted up to the corner where she and Micky always stood, and when she found that Micky wasn't there, she turned and whinnied.

"Come on," yelled Dad. "Get back in, all of you."

They piled into the car, Mum in the front struggling to get through to the number, and the other three in the back.

"No signal here, but I'll keep trying!" said Mum and hit the buttons again.

Rosie was silent as Dad started the engine but Charlie was crying openly now.

"He's mine! At last he was going to be mine and now I might never see him again…and if I don't, I'll die! I can't bear it..." Her sobs were growing louder and her thin shoulders were shaking.

"Charlie, come on now," said Tom, "You must stay calm. If Micky's to be yours, then he needs you to help him. He needs you more than any of us, so you must stay calm. Everything's goin' to be fine."

The look on his face was less reassuring than his words, and Rosie guessed this wasn't the first time he'd followed a horse up this winding lane. In spite of everything that was happening it struck her how different Tom was from the rest of his family. 'I'd like to meet his mother one day,' she thought. 'He must take after her!'

Suddenly Mum shouted: "It's ringing!"

Dad slowed a little and all their eyes were glued to the mobile.

"Oh, heavens, no reply!" she cried.

"There must be someone there," Tom said. "Ma Phelan doesn't go out much."

Dad revved the engine. Charlie opened her mouth to renew her wailing, but he forestalled her by shouting, "Keep trying Mum. And Tom, tell me which way to go!"

***

They went straight inland towards the town, through the centre and out on to another winding road that climbed slowly towards the distant hills.

"Mr Phelan's place is about four miles along here," Tom said.

"Four miles!" Charlie cried in horror. "Four miles more!"

Mum whispered to Dad, "I only hope those aren't 'Irish' miles! Charlie won't last out!"

Dad muttered through clenched teeth: "None of us will if she goes on making that noise." He suddenly barked at his younger daughter, "Charlotte if you can't stop that, I shall leave you here under a hedge, and I shall leave Micky to his fate. Be quiet or you'll make me crash this car. I'm warning you!"

Poor Dad, no-one ever took much notice of his threats, so Rosie tried an old trick of her own. She took one of Charlie's hands and gripped it really tight. "You've got ten seconds to shut up," she hissed, "before I break all your fingers...one…two…thr…"

It worked. Charlie took a shuddering breath and closed her mouth. She then just sat and stared fixedly at the road ahead… But she left her hand in Rosie's.

The silence in the car was broken moments later by Tom.

"Ah. No. There's me da." He threw up an arm, pointing. "He must be on his way back."

They looked ahead to where the red transit van and battered trailer were snaking towards them, bouncing between the hedges, about half a mile ahead. As soon as he found a passing place, Dad pulled off the narrow road as far as he could.

"Quick kids, get down out of sight. I don't think he knows this car. I hope not anyway."

Mum, in a flash of inspiration, hissed at Rosie: "The binoculars, quick."

Rosie's hand waved above the seat and grabbed them off the back shelf. Dad held them to his face and Mum buried her nose in a map.

"Has he still got Micky? What's he doing with him?" Charlie was nearly hysterical again, and Rosie had to clamp her hands over her sister's mouth as the van approached.

"Oh dear, what if he sees us?" Mum crossed all her fingers as she held up the tourist guide...

...And that's all Seamus Keenan saw. Just a pair of tourists getting in his way – as far as he was concerned that was what tourists usually did – and he hardly gave them a second glance as his van rattled past. As it did so, all eyes inside the car went to the rear view mirror. The trailer was empty.

***

Micky stood on the bare concrete, tied to a metal ring. He didn't like any of this. There was a strange smell in the air. He'd been dragged out of the stable, just as he'd recovered enough to pick at his hay, and then the awful man had forced him into the trailer again, and driven here like a demon. Micky was drenched with sweat from his horrendous journey and once again he was scared. He didn't know what was going to happen next, he just knew he didn't want to be here.

Jim Phelan was an old racing man, an ex-jockey, who'd been quite successful in his youth, and horses had always been his life. Now he looked at Micky and sighed. Once or twice he'd managed to find homes for unwanted animals but you couldn't do it with them all, and sometimes he could see a horse had had enough, but this was a youngster, a Connie, and he'd always had a soft spot for Connies. At times like this Jim really didn't like his job. He hadn't got much time for Seamus Keenan either. He was no horseman, and not even much of a barman – too fond of the stuff himself! But business was business.

"You can't be more than three," he said to Micky, and he stroked his nose. "Ah well, best get on with it." He took the special key out of his pocket and headed purposefully towards his office.

The car was speeding on. Charlie's wails grew louder, and Rosie was really struggling not to join her.

Tom said nothing, but his mind was racing. Sometimes Phelan kept them a few days, trying to sell them on, and sometimes he didn't. Which was he doing this time? They were about to find out.

"It's up here on the right," he said, leaning forward between the two front seats and pointing. "It's through that gap in the hedge, you can see the house there...and there's the barn, that's where they..." Dad stepped sharply on the brake and silenced Tom with a shake of his head.

The car gathered speed again and roared up the lane towards the ugly concrete building with a corrugated iron roof. There was a man moving around the side, and he had something in his hand.

"Mr Phelan! Mr Phelan!" Tom had the window down and was almost climbing out of it. He leapt out of the door the moment Dad stopped the car.

"Mr Phelan," Tom was tearing towards the man. "Don't... the grey pony...these people, they want him. They'll buy him off youse."

The man's head turned. "Ah, is it you now, Tom. Why on earth didn't ya da tell me that? Bringing the poor little fella all the way out here, and him in such a state. Oh dear me. Poor little chap."

By now, the whole family was standing beside Tom. Rosie burst into sobs. She couldn't control herself any longer, and she and Charlie clung together for a moment. Then the smaller girl pulled away from her sister, and they all looked on helplessly as she threw herself at the startled Irishman and began to pummel him with her fists. After a moment, he managed to get hold of her and, as the furious attack petered out, he held the small figure at arms' length and spoke to her gently.

"Hey now, hold on. Now did I say that he wasn't here any more? I did not. But I think he'll need some real tender love and care to keep him going. Now wait a minute little misses, and I'll fetch him for you."

He raised his hand, "Oh no, they'd better not come in there, Tom. Take them up to the house and I'll bring him over. We can tie him up by me donkeys – just 'til ya da can come and fetch him back." Everyone started talking at once and, through the hubbub, Jim Phelan gathered that Seamus Keenan was the last person who should be told about any of this.

A little later, over a cup of tea and some of Ma Phelan's scones – "scones to die for" Mum sighed – it was agreed that nobody should be told anything. Dad and Jim went out into the garden for "a little business chat" and Ma P, who'd been getting in the washing when they tried to phone, barely had time to refill Mum's cup before they were back, all smiles, with Jim folding something away into his back pocket.

"But where on earth can we put him for now?" asked Mum, anxiously, stirring in an extra spoonful of sugar to settle her nerves.

Ma poked Jim with her slipper, and he looked first at her, and then from one worried face to another.

"Oh well," he said at last." My old donkeys are gettin' too fat anyway. Mebbes they could share a bit of their grass with Micky 'til youse can get him all fixed up."

Charlie moved over and put her hand into Jim's.

"I'm really sorry I beat you up just now," she grinned up at him. "You're not nearly as bad as I thought."

By this time Rosie couldn't speak at all, so she just beamed at him. Tom hitched his chair a little closer to Rosie, and Mum buttered another scone for Dad and put it on his plate. They clinched the deal with a tot of Irish Whiskey from a bottle Jim kept in the coal scuttle. Jim and Ma P, Mum and Dad, Tom, and even the girls had a tiny nip, to drink the health of their pony – Micky the Connemara.

***

Five days later two vehicles checked in at the docks in Cork. One was a family saloon with three people in it. They seemed to be arguing about something. The other was a small, somewhat scruffy, blue horse box with a scratch down one side and a wing mirror fastened on with baler twine. In the front were the burly driver and a boy with black hair and bright blue eyes.

He had a suitcase beside him and in his pocket a letter of introduction from an old Irish jockey to a racehorse trainer in Sussex. Between them sat a small girl in a boy's shirt, clutching some registration papers from a smart Connemara stud, with a very determined look on her face.

In the back was a fine strapping two-year-old thoroughbred destined for the same Sussex stable. And behind him, hock-deep in straw and swathed in protective bandages, battle-scarred and apprehensive, but still feeling better than he'd ever felt in his life before, was a thirteen hand iron-grey pony with white spots on his back.

The Welsh Cob

The Welsh Cob

The girl on the pony looked down at her mother and grinned. "You must be going deaf, Mum." She poked her mother with the toe of her boot. "I said: this is the one I want." "You're crazy!" The little woman's ginger curls bounced about as she spoke. She looked up at her daughter, and frowned, "She's much too big. You know what they say about mares, and Welsh Cobs can be pig-headed sometimes..."

"I don't care Mum." Clare was sitting astride a bay roan Welsh Section D of daunting proportions. She was only just over 14 hands high, but there was a lot of her – big strong shoulders, a hefty neck, and four people could have sat round and eaten tea off her back! "She's so lovely..." If Clare had said that once this afternoon, she'd said it twenty times. "She's big and solid and hairy, just the sort I like." She dropped the reins, leant down and fastened her arms round the mare's neck. "And she's ever so comfy – like an armchair. You'll love riding her as well!" "Yes, but will she do what you want to do?" said Mum. "How would she go at Pony Club rallies, or Camp? I can't exactly see her in the dressage team! It would be silly to get a pony that won't do all the things you like. Honestly darling, do think sensibly. Let's sleep on it. There's no rush." "There is, Mum, there is," Clare tightened her grip and the pony shook her head in protest. "I want to take her home and I don't need to sleep on anything. I've ridden her twice now, and she's what I want, I'm sure. And anyway, I hate dressage." Clare's eyes were gleaming with

enthusiasm, and her lips were just beginning to set in the determined line that her mum knew so well. She was her father's daughter all right, and it was his mother who was at the back of all this.

Granny Miles and Clare had always been close. When Clare was small and fell off, which was quite often, it was Granny M who calmly picked her up and plonked her back on again. She had died a year ago, and left Clare some money in her will: '*to buy her the pony she wants, when she's 12 and riding properly.*' Well, in the five weeks since Clare's birthday in August they'd looked at a lot of ponies, in all the horsy magazines and on-line, but this one was out of a local paper. **Brilliant hunting pony 14.1 Welsh Cob for sale** – it had said.

"What will we do with a hunting pony?" Mum had muttered as Clare dragged her to the car. "We don't hunt." "It's a Welsh Cob and I've always wanted one. That other cobby thing we looked at was gorgeous but I couldn't afford him. This one's cheaper so I'll have some money left over to help pay the bills." So here they were again, standing in the tatty dealer's yard round the back of a dreary industrial estate. Several horses and ponies of different shapes and sizes were looking dolefully out of boxes.

All of them were for sale. Clare and her mum had tried the mare yesterday and Clare really liked her. Mum wasn't so sure. She thought Clare looked like a pea on a drum, sitting up there. But it was Clare's money, so today they'd come back to take her out on the road. The pony was as good as gold in the traffic, and now a rather creepy-looking man was waiting impatiently for them to make up their minds. He'd said he was selling the cob for a friend who'd got pregnant and was giving up riding, and that the pony was "sadly for sale". That was always a good line, he thought, nice and reassuring for the people buying. Actually she was quite a decent sort this mare, only eight years old, good looking in a hefty sort of way – lots of hair everywhere.

She had a bit of a look in her eye but so had quite a lot of Welshes. He hoped they'd settle it now and he could get his cut of the cash. He was dying for a drink and it was getting late. But they'd probably want to sleep on it. Most women did.

Clare swung her leg over the pommel of the saddle and slid down. "Honestly Mum, she's great, and I want a pony I can work on, not a push-button job who does it all for me. Please. You've seen how good she is in the stable. Oh just look at her face! Mummy, I *must* have her." Clare put on her 'remember-how-cute-I-was-when-I-was-small' voice and smile, and as usual, she got away with it. Mum sighed as she turned and looked again at the pony. She had to agree the mare's face was pretty, with nice large eyes, and now she was looking back at them enquiringly.

"Well, we can't have her on trial," she said, "so if she doesn't work out you'll have to be responsible for re-homing her. I've told you what I think but I suppose it's up to you. The money's

yours, and Granny Miles always did like hairy ponies. I expect she'll be looking down and grinning. I just wish she was here to help us, I've got a feeling we're going to need it." "Mum I love you." Clare flung her arms round her, then dashed to the car, dug into Mum's bag and came back with the chequebook and pen.

"Hang on, Clare. We can't take her now. Don't forget we lent the trailer to the Jacksons, so Amy could go to Prince Philip Cup. We'll have to wait 'til Friday at the earliest." As she put away her pen, she moved towards the car, and nearly fell over the man who suddenly appeared at her elbow.

"No trouble, mam," he said. "I'll box her over to you first thing in the morning." He glanced at his watch. He could just make the bank if these two got a move on. It was a lot easier if a child took a real fancy to one. They could almost always get round their parents, and this girl was no exception. They put the pony back into the stable, Clare hanging over the door and babbling happily to her about how much she was going to love her new home, then the deal was struck and they drove out of the yard. Once they were out of sight, the man gave the cheque a little kiss and tucked it into his wallet. 'One born every minute,' he thought. 'Luckily for me.'

* * *

Dad was trying to watch the breakfast news before he left for work. He liked this time of the day, as long as nobody wanted him to decide anything, talk about anything serious or do anything else grown-up! Clare's brother Jack was struggling with the holiday project that he'd left until the very last minute as usual. The two dogs were in bed. The Jack Russell was fast asleep in the middle and the old Labrador was curled round the edge, trying to look as if that was where he wanted to be. They had a bed each, but every morning found them both squashed up in one of them.

Clare had been up since six doing up the pony's box, refilling the water trough in the field and checking the fences, even though

Misty, Mum's old thoroughbred, and the two donkeys had been out in the paddocks for years. Now she was back in the kitchen and under everybody's feet. "We've still got a week of the holidays left," she said. "We'll settle her in quietly over the autumn, and I'll do a few rallies at half term and Christmas, and by next summer and Camp she'll be the perfect pony. You wait and see."

"All right Clare, good. I'll look forward to that," Dad said vaguely, spreading another slice of toast with his own home-made marmalade. He was thinking to himself, 'Another blooming pony – thank you so much, Lisa, wife of mine!' Life was hard. He'd always been surrounded by pony-mad women: his mother, his sister, his wife, and now his daughter. Only he and Jack were relatively normal with other interests apart from horses. Though he couldn't deny he'd been quite fond of Clare's first pony Bertie, a little New Forest-cross. It was a pity she'd grown out of him. He'd been no trouble, and cheap to keep as well. Pity daughters had to get bigger. Jack wished they'd all be quiet, so he could concentrate on 'The Significance of Global Warming, and how it could affect our Local Environment' – especially the state of the school football pitch (Which he wouldn't be using for a while if this project wasn't in by the first day of term!) He was fed-up with all the fuss over this new pony, and it wasn't even here yet. He'd ordered an iPad with his money from Granny M, and just had it delivered – easy. It didn't need feeding, taking out in lousy weather or mucking out. Jack regarded all these activities as a complete waste of time and effort. All the girls he knew were daft over horses. Girls were stupid it seemed to him. He stumped off upstairs with his huge bowl of cereal and a piece of bread clamped between his teeth.

Clare was cramming cornflakes into her mouth when a horn tooted in the road outside. She dashed out, followed by the dogs, and opened the gate. An old brown lorry pulled in and the creepy man climbed down. He opened the back and Clare ran up the ramp. He untied the pony, who appeared to be asleep, and the excited girl took the lead rope off him. She led the mare down towards her dad, who was staring in amazement. "Dad this is Gwynnan Sandpiper. Sandy this is my dad, Robert Miles." Dad closed his mouth, eventually, and spoke: "Well if you're going by the weight I'd say you'd got good value for your money," he said. "I expected a bigger pony, but I didn't expect a juggernaut!" "It's nothing to do with me," said Mum after she'd collected Sandy's paperwork and seen the lorry out into the road. "This is Clare's choice and her responsibility, but this pony must weigh twice as much as Bertie did, probably more. I think she's mad."

With that she marched the dogs out for a walk, leaving Clare gazing lovingly over the door of Sandy's box. Dad went off to work wondering how much the new pony was going to eat, and Jack who had been peering out of an upstairs window shut himself away in his room in case Clare should need any help.

***

They let Sandy have two or three days to settle in. She was in a small field next to the others at first, and there was much squealing over the fence, Sandy with her ears back and her top lip curling as she investigated her new companions. When she did go in with them and the first flurry of nips and flying hooves was over, the pecking order was soon established. And guess who was at the top? Sandy ruled the roost and Misty followed amiably behind. He was much too old and wise to make a fuss, especially as the donkeys didn't always let him in the shelter at night: it was getting colder, and it would be nice to have something big to stand behind when the wind blew.

Sandy was good to catch, and she stood like a lamb when anything needed to be done. All in all, she was very easy to look after. She didn't make a fuss if she was tied up on her own, or left in the stable when the others were out in the field.

The farrier didn't bother tie her up at all, and she stood with her foot up on his tripod, head drooping and eyes half closed with a "do-what-you-like-to-me" expression on her face, as he did her shoes. "Well this is a change from Bertie the fidget," he said, grinning and showing the gaps in his teeth. (He used to be a three-day eventer and had taken a few falls in his time.) "If they were all like her, I'd get home in time for an early tea every day."

Clare beamed. It was all working out perfectly. Sandy was going to be the best pony ever. She'd ridden her in the fields for a few days until she settled in, and now decided to go out for a potter, with Mum on Misty.

"I'll go in front," Mum said. "Keep close to me 'til we turn off the road."

They went out of the gate and Sandy walked placidly behind the old thoroughbred. They lived on quite a busy road. Several cars and two or three lorries of varying size roared up, changed gear and then crawled past the two horses. In spite of his advancing years, Misty still tensed up when a big noisy truck came close, especially if it had those horrid hissy airbrakes, but Sandy hardly flicked an ear, and Clare's confidence grew with every stride. Even so, they were both glad to turn off onto the bridleway. The trees were beginning to turn red and gold and everything looked lovely in the autumn sunshine. A family of pheasants skittered off the path at the sight of them, and once again Sandy was less perturbed than Misty, who veered to the side and snorted. Mum laughed. She was used to him and there wasn't a mean bone in his old body. He was just a bit highly strung. After all, he had been bred to be a racehorse.

Clare was feeling rather superior by now. There's nothing like a bombproof pony for making you look a super rider!

"Can't we trot now, Mum?" she asked, gathering up her reins as she spoke. "I'm dying to let her go. I'll be in front shall I? In case there are any more birds who want to commit suicide?" "OK." Mum agreed and gave Misty a squeeze.

* * *

Clare never could explain how she ended up on the ground under Sandy's nose. One moment Sandy was steaming along in her fast Welsh trot – the next minute she wasn't. She swerved violently, stopped dead, and deposited Clare on her bottom. Neither Clare nor Mum could see anything frightening, just trees on one side and a farm gate on the other. Sandy wandered to the nearest bush and started eating. Mum jumped off and picked Clare up. "You're OK, the ground's not too hard, so no harm done, eh? I'll give you a leg up and we'll just walk the rest of the way. But what on earth did she spook at? And she certainly didn't give you any warning, bad girl!" Poor Clare. Her backside was sore and her confidence dented. The worst thing was she'd be wondering all the way home if Sandy was going to do it again, but she was determined not to let Mum see that, because she knew what she'd say...

Sandy munched calmly at the oak leaves clamped between her jaws, then moved reluctantly forward as Clare gathered up the reins again. "It's just because all this is new to her," she said, as they turned rather thankfully into their gate. "I expect she's really nervous with the strain of changing homes." "She doesn't look very nervous to me." Dad was watching Sandy rolling luxuriantly in the only muddy patch in the paddock. "And she's certainly not off her feed. She's going cost me a fortune. She'd better not do things like that too often."

***

But she did. Clare began to get the knack of sticking on, but these invisible terrors lurked on almost every ride. On the road she was angelic, but once in the woods or fields, Sandy would leap in the air or swerve sideways for no good reason that anybody could see. It was very disconcerting for the person on top. And her speciality consisted of bunching up her large body with no advance warning, humping her back and scuttling forwards, almost on tiptoe, at high speed. This manoeuvre had Clare flying over her tail more than once. Then Sandy would wander calmly off and start eating, or just look down at her rider, as if surprised to see her in a heap on the ground. On these occasions Clare didn't know whether to laugh or cry.

Her other trick was less unseating but even more annoying. She would just stop. She planted all four feet, and wouldn't move. Clare kicked and shouted at her, and was reduced to tears sometimes when she was riding alone. All this she kept to herself because, when she wasn't being awful, Sandy was an angel and Clare loved her. Also she had chosen her and wasn't going to admit she'd been wrong. She decided that if Mum saw any bruises, when she was in the bath, or getting ready for bed, she'd say they were from playing hockey at school. But there was just one *other* problem. Sandy was perfectly happy to go into a horsebox. She was obviously used to travelling in one of those. The Miles's trailer was quite another matter. Perhaps she thought it was beneath her. It certainly wasn't too small, as Misty had plenty of headroom. Maybe she didn't need any reason to dislike it. But dislike it she did! She would stop at the bottom of the ramp just when they thought she was going to walk in, swing her large bottom to the side and lean gently backwards. Sandy's ears would flop sideways and she'd look at Clare with one of her 'what's-the-point-of-all-this' faces, as she rested a back foot. There wasn't much Clare could do. She couldn't pull or push her in. She was too big for that, and a broom head across her back-side simply made her lean back more heavily until Clare's arms gave out, or the handle snapped. It was all very tiring. Mum helped when she could and they gradually got the better of her by placing the trailer alongside the wall, with the hedge close by so she'd nowhere else to go but in. Then a lunge rein on each side stopped her from turning, if you held on very tight that is. And a bucket of nuts made the trailer much more inviting. But all this took time – and patience. Getting cross was no help at all, in fact Sandy seemed to quite enjoy getting everyone's attention.

"Good job it's football this term," gasped Mum, as she was hanging on to the lunge rope,

"Dad hasn't really seen this performance. He's too busy with Jack and the team."

"Don't tell him him," said Clare. "Please Mum, I know she'll get better at loading. It's just she's not used to the trailer. I understand how she feels." Mum thought, 'It's lucky for Sandy that Clare's so loyal. I'd have had enough by now.' Dad had certainly noticed one thing. After five years of shouting at his wife and daughter that they were "going to be late for the show", they seemed to have got the message at last. Nowadays they were always early leaving, so he and Jack could have a nice peaceful lie-in at the weekend.

***

The day they took Sandy to her first Pony Club Rally they were *very* early. Nobody wants to be late for a rally, and if you've got a new pony it's embarrassing to arrive all hot and bothered when everyone else is mounted and waiting.

They packed the car the night before and lined up the trailer before Clare got Sandy out of her stable. She had all her fingers crossed. Sandy went straight in – of course – and so they had masses of time to spare. They didn't want to keep her standing in there, and they didn't dare take her out again. So, even though Mum drove very slowly, they arrived at the District Commissioner's farm about an hour too soon. Two of the instructors were there, setting out the various arenas, but no other horses yet. Mum had the whole field to park in, and didn't have to struggle to get the trailer into an awkward space.

"That's one good thing, thank goodness," she exclaimed to Clare. "I always make a mess of it when other people are looking. So I'm glad we're early for once." "Thanks to Sandy," Clare pointed out, and Mum was forced to agree. Sandy came out of the trailer quietly and was quite happy to be tied up, so long as she could reach the grass. Clare finished getting the shavings out of her tail and oiled her hooves. The pony was quiet and relaxed. She always travelled quite happily – once you got her in. That was what made Mum so mad. She hardly ever seemed stressed. She was just awkward when she felt like it. And you couldn't even rely on her to be awkward about the same thing twice, so you never knew where you were with her, or what she was going to do next! 'Bloomin' Welsh Cobs,' Mum thought. 'Bloomin' mares.' Clare got on Sandy and wandered about the edge of the large field. Mum went off to ask which ride they would be in. Jill Johnson, the Pony Club District Commissioner – DC for short – had got the list. This list always caused trouble. Someone always thought they should be in a different ride to the one they'd been put in. The top ones, with the big horses, were going to do dressage proper, while the three younger rides were just having lessons, and doing a few jumps in the school later.

The DC was in her fifties. She was a kindly woman, but she wouldn't stand any nonsense – from the children, the ponies, *or* the parents. She sometimes thought the parents were twice as much trouble as the other two put together. Her three sons had all done well on ponies and her youngest was now competing with considerable success. He had his sights on Badminton with his clever young horse, so Jill expected quite a lot of the Pony Club children.

Courtesy, consideration and courage. That was her motto. **And determination.**

Her branch was not for the faint-hearted. She looked across at Clare Miles on Sandy and sighed. The pony looked as if it had a mind of its own, and although Clare was a lovely girl, she was neither the toughest nor the bravest of riders. Jill had hoped a new pony would be the making of her, but she had a nasty feeling that...'but we'll wait and see', the DC thought, and turned to Mum: "I've put her in the second ride. I thought Rose would be the best instructor for her as it's the pony's first rally. How's she been going at home? Quite a size isn't she?" Mum nodded and smiled. She never knew quite what to say to the DC. She'd not been in the Pony Club herself, but Clare enjoyed it all, and had learned a lot so far. Bertie had been an old hand, and she'd taken him to three junior camps and had a great time. The inside of the tent bore the evidence of that when they came to fetch her home. Jack said he'd never seen so many sweet wrappers and crisp packets under one ground sheet.

"Girls are much greedier than boys. No wonder she's got spots," he had jeered, and Clare had clouted him a couple of times. In fact she hit her brother more often and harder than she'd ever smacked a pony. Mum looked across at her daughter now and waved. Other trailers and boxes were parking up now and there were people everywhere. The rally was getting under way at last. Girls in jackets and Pony Club ties were getting into their groups, and ponies of all shapes and sizes were walking and trotting around, with most of their riders more or less in control. Rose Macintyre climbed out of her battered Land Rover – leaving the windows open for her dogs – and hitched up her elderly tracksuit bottoms. She enjoyed teaching children, but always slightly dreaded the moment she was told whose child was in her class. In twenty years she'd hardly ever had an entirely contented row of mothers watching their offspring perform; there was at least one troublemaker. Still, this lot didn't look too bad. She looked at the list and saw that Clare Miles was in her group. Someone said she'd got her new pony at last. She squinted through her glasses as the ponies lined up. There was a large brownish one on the end. She cleaned her specs on her sleeve and looked again. 'Oh good gracious,' she thought. 'What on earth is that?'

* * *

"Push her on," Rose said. "You must make her do what you want her to. Give her a smack to show you mean it."

Sandy was refusing to move out of the line. Rose had had them all trotting and cantering to the back of the ride, and Sandy had done everything so far. Now that they were lined up for some individual work, she'd gone off to sleep and saw no reason to wake up and do it all over again on her own.

“Come along Clare. Get cross with her.” But Clare got upset instead, and sat without moving. She’d wanted everyone to say how beautiful Sandy was, and how lucky she was to have her, but although her friends said she was “nice” and “quite cute”, they’d all gone into the next ride up, and she’d seen two of them looking over and laughing when Sandy was dozing just now and resting a large back leg. Even Rose, who’d taught her for so long, had only said: “Well, you’ve certainly got your hands full now, but I dare say you’ll grow into her.” That’s what most people said and Clare was fed up with it. She suddenly gave Sandy a great boot in the ribs and the mare moved calmly forward and broke into a trot.

“Well done,” shouted Rose. “Do a circle and then go large, canter at C and go round once. Don’t let her break back to trot until you want her to.” Clare did this without a problem, Sandy managed to stay awake and they went off to do some jumping. She even went over a few small jumps quite sweetly, mostly from a trot, but she jumped them. Clare was pink in the face with pleasure when Rose said, "Well done, good girl." She walked Sandy over to the trailer and gave her half a packet of Polos. Sandy dropped her lower lip and did one of her "nothing-to-it" faces, before having another quick pick of grass.

***

"She just nodded off," Clare said as they were driving home, "It was quite hot. I was half asleep too. You can't blame her. Rose said she needs lots of flatwork, and I'm sure she's right. I'd like to go to one of Declan's rallies, if we could get in. Could you ask? Will you? I can pay for it!" "I thought you hated dressage," Mum replied, sticking her hand out of the window and indicating right. 'I must get the electrics on the towbar checked,' she was thinking, as Clare gabbled on.

"I've changed my mind, Mum. It would be so good for her, make her much more supple. And more obedient maybe," she added, hopefully. The next day, Mum phoned the Pony Club dressage organiser. Everyone wanted to have a lesson with Declan. He made dressage such fun. His lessons were very popular, so Mum didn't hold out much hope that they would get in. But Declan had a bit of a soft spot for Clare, and her mum, too, with her wild hair and lop-sided grin. He'd got to know them when they took on old Bertie, who'd been his own first pony. He liked the way that they could laugh at themselves when things went wrong – like the time Clare shot off the side as Bertie whizzed round the bending poles in lead-rein gymkhana. They just laughed and had a go at the mug race. So, Declan decided to give Clare twenty minutes on her own at the start of the morning session. When she came into the school his jaw dropped in mock horror. "My god. Is that the Titanic?" he asked in his lilting Irish voice. "Or is it the iceberg that sank the Titanic?"

Clare laughed. He pulled such a funny face, she couldn't help it. She and Sandy had a lovely twenty minutes. The pony went happily round on a nice long rein and when Declan said, "Steady on Clare, I think she nearly came down on the bit just then," she laughed again. It was as if Sandy liked him too, she was so relaxed and calm. As she came out of the school, Clare realised that two of the older girls had been watching with their mothers, both of whom were Pony Club Committee Members and rather serious about dressage. She was really glad that Sandy had been on her best behaviour and hadn't spooked or stopped dead and dumped her off. She and Mum had parked in a little space on the lane behind the school, away from the yard and out of sight. Mum had turned the trailer round and now was hoping that Sandy wouldn't be naughty about going back in. But of course she was.

She wouldn't go anywhere near the ramp – just planted herself three or four metres away. The lunge rope made no difference, and they were still there when the next two people drove by. Clare pretended she was checking the headcollar, and then when the road was empty she turned Sandy and tried to run her towards the ramp. But she ducked out, pulled the lead rope from Clare's hand and got loose. Then she trotted slowly off – lip curled –alongside the outer fence of the school, stopping only when she was in full view of Declan and all the other people.

"Remember what I said Clare: she's your responsibility." Mum leant into the Land Rover for the flask of coffee. "I'm not catching her!"

Clare bent double and crept along the hedge. When she reached the pony she tried to make a discreet grab for the rope, but Sandy would have none of that and shied along the path with a rattle of hooves.

"Loose horse!" shouted one of the Committee Members and started to climb through the fence to the rescue. "Ah now, that'll be Clare behind the hedge, won't it Clare?" Declan called. And Clare straightened up, scarlet and breathless, and gave a rather unconvincing smile. "Are you all right?" The bossy woman was halfway through the fence now, but Declan checked her progress by saying, "If Clare can't catch the Titanic before she hits something I'd be very surprised. Lucky there's not much ice round here today, eh Clare?" Nobody else knew what on earth the mad Irishman was talking about, but the woman climbed back, and as she did so, Declan winked at Clare and grinned.

She eventually caught Sandy who was definitely playing to her audience, tossing her head to avoid any outstretched hand, trotting just out of reach, then stopping to eat the hedge voraciously as if she had never been fed. The audience, of course, was riveted, and gave Clare a round of applause when she finally got hold of Sandy, and led her off out of sight.

***

Jack came in the gate on his bike. "Have a good lesson. How was the mad Irishman?" He looked surprised when Clare dashed into Sandy's box and slammed the door shut after her. By now Dad had heard the story from Mum and he laughed aloud. "Poor old Clare," he chuckled. "What will Sandy do next? That pony's a horror." "What can I do? Clare loves her." Mum sighed resignedly. She put the kettle on for a cup of tea, and then she just burst out laughing too.

***

The next thing was less of a joke. The Pony Club have lots of different things you can have a go at, and this was a cross-country practice at Mrs Brent-Osborn's place.

Mrs B.O. as everyone called her – even her own husband – had seen Sandy out hunting in the past. She recognised her at once and came up to Mum and said: "I've followed this mare a couple of times. She can jump! You'll have a lot of fun with her. Jolly good to see her again." Mum smiled and nodded. She knew that people laughed at Mrs B.O. and some said she was a terrible snob, but Mum always tried to be fair. "I don't know her," she said to Clare once, "so I can't say what she's like. She lets the Pony Club onto her cross-country course, and helps at shows and things. That's kind of her, anyway." Mum was secretly in awe of people like Mrs B.O. They never doubted that they knew best. "That must make life so simple," she sighed. Still, it was good to hear someone praising Sandy. She passed it on to Clare as she gave her a leg up and Clare was delighted.

Unfortunately, Clare's instructor that day was not someone who liked Welsh Cobs, or any other hairy ponies.

Mrs Janet Franks was one of those women who never seemed to have a hair out of place. She didn't believe ponies should have a hair out of place either. All hers were clipped and trimmed to within an inch of their lives, and it was more than their lives were worth to step out of line when she was around. She disapproved of long manes and feathery feet, and this great lump in front of her now was a shambles. She also thought the rider was feeble in the extreme.

There were five ponies in the group, and Sandy was the biggest by far. All the others were seasoned campaigners. Most of them had had several small owners, and they knew the ropes. The easiest option today was to jump all the obstacles with the minimum of fuss, and that way everyone got home quicker for tea. The first fence was a simple log pile, not very big. Mrs Franks said: "Right then, who's going first?"

A very small girl, who was the youngest in a large competitive family, sailed over on the family schoolmaster, and made it look easy. Clare was feeling rather confident after what Mrs B.O. had said about Sandy, so she went next. She trotted off, turned her round and came towards the logs. "No, no, no! Stop!" Mrs Franks glared at Clare. "What are you doing? Don't you know you must get a nice rhythmic canter to an obstacle? Go round and get it cantering. Use your stick. That's what it's for. Come on! The others are waiting."

Clare flushed and tried again, not using her stick, just squeezing firmly with her lower leg. But Sandy didn't feel like cantering. She much preferred to trot – especially over such a stupid little jump – so that's what she did. In the end, Mrs Franks made Clare wait until all the others had jumped and then finally allowed her to trot over it. "But I hope you can get a canter out of it soon, preferably today!" She had a horrid sarcastic voice, and Sandy put her ears back as she trotted past her and pulled one of her worst faces.

Clare hated people calling horses "it" and secretly patted Sandy, and whispered, "If she talks to you like that again, you can bite her if you like." This thought made her laugh, and she felt a bit better. She looked up to see that Mum was coming over to watch. They did a rustic spread next, and Sandy did canter this time as the jump was bigger and slightly uphill. Clare was glad that Mum saw her clear it nicely two or three times.

Then they moved on to the other side of the field.

***

Mrs B.O. had all sorts of different obstacles: ditches, logs, banks and two water jumps, one with a drop into it and an easier one you could approach from several directions. This was their next fence. It involved a little drop into about fifteen centimetres of water. The other groups had been there first and the water was now muddy and uninviting. The weather was also getting much colder, and Clare gave a little shiver as she looked down into the murky water. She really hoped she wouldn't fall off into it. Sandy decided that if Clare didn't want to leap into a dangerous dark hole full of water, then she certainly wasn't going to bother. A voice behind Mum made them both start. "That's funny," said Mrs B.O. "I've seen her jump water lots of times!" 'Oh no,' thought Clare, 'She would have to come round now!' At that very moment Sandy was going backwards rather fast. "Well…" Mrs B.O. ploughed on, blissfully unaware of the effect her words were having. "The woman who used to ride her gave me a lead more than once. I wonder what's got into her today?" She looked up at Clare, then shrugged, and walked away. Clare wished they'd all leave her alone. She just wanted to get herself organised without people nagging at her. She was sure Sandy thought there was something horrid in the water and if only she could show her there wasn't, then Sandy would jump in. It was only about a thirty-centimetre drop. Mrs Franks finally lost patience. "I've got four other children to get round these jumps," she complained. "This hairy thing is useless!"...and so is the child, she nearly added, but stopped herself just in time. "Oh, for goodness sake, leave it," she said. "We'll go on to the next." Mum could see Clare was getting upset again, and so she gingerly approached Mrs Franks. "Umm...do you think...could we stay on our own," she asked, "and try to get her in? We don't want to hold up the lesson for the others."

"Oh, all right," was the grumpy reply. "But make sure she does it. That pony needs to learn who's boss," and Mrs Franks led the others off to tackle the wall. When they were alone, Mum rolled up her trousers, took off her shoes and socks and jumped into the pool.

"The things I do for you Clare," she grumbled. The water was freezing. "Come on, you toad." She pulled at Sandy's rein. "Look, it's quite safe, you silly idiot." But by now Sandy had decided that jumping down there was definitely not on the agenda for today. Mum went behind her and tried to shoo her forward, stinging her bare feet on some nettles as she did so. She climbed back down into the pool again and splashed about encouragingly to show Sandy it wasn't frightening. Suddenly she started to see the funny side of all this, and at last Clare began to grin too, at the sight of her mad mother splashing about and laughing in the freezing cold. They were so engrossed they didn't see Mrs Franks come back, and both jumped when she suddenly shouted: "This is ridiculous, give me your stick."

"What for?" Clare cried. "I'm going get this horse into that water and I'll whack it if I have to." She grabbed at Clare's stick, but Clare held on and cried out "Don't hit my pony!" She stood up in her stirrups and held her stick high above her head, out of reach of Mrs Franks waving arm. Mum stood in the water, staring at Clare in surprise and admiration. She finally opened her mouth to back up her daughter, but then Sandy joined in the excitement. She half turned, and one of her hind legs slipped down the bank. She tried to regain her balance, lost the other hind leg and slid backwards, into the water. Mum had no time to get out of the way, and as Sandy's hind foot landed on hers, she felt her toes break like the squares snapping off a bar of chocolate. She let out a high-pitched yell. Sandy leapt out of the water like a scalded cat and then there was a strange silence. By the time Mum managed to crawl up on to the bank, Mrs Franks had disappeared. Sandy was looking stressed, her eyes rolling and sweat breaking out on her neck, and Clare was very pale. She jumped off and helped Mum to hobble back to the trailer. To their amazement Sandy went straight in and stood there like a lamb.

"She knows you can't help me," Clare said. "She understands how we feel, I know she does." Mrs B.O. had been told about the accident and she phoned Dad, who arrived soon afterwards in a taxi, and drove them home. Then he and Mum went straight on to A and E.

Clare felt awful. Poor Mum! But it had been an accident. She knew Sandy would never hurt anyone deliberately. If anyone was to blame it was that horrid Mrs Franks. She put Sandy to bed and fed everyone, and was coming in the back door when the sound of voices made her pause. Mum and Dad were back and they were arguing. "She's a liability, and she's dangerous, and this proves it." Dad sounded very angry. "Look at your poor foot, in plaster. That bloody pony will have to go, and the sooner the better." Without stopping to think Clare dashed in. "It was that awful woman," she shouted fiercely. "It wasn't Sandy's fault. That woman frightened her and she slipped. She didn't mean to step on Mum. Please Dad – give her another chance. You could tell she was sorry. She knew she'd hurt Mum. Please Dad." "Horses," Jack butted in. "Stupid unpredictable things, give me bikes any day, they don't answer back." "Shut up Jack." Clare lunged at him and that settled it. Dad sent her up to bed and she cried herself to sleep. Between her sobs she told herself over and over: "I can get her going, I know I can – if I can just find out what makes her tick. *She isn't bad*, I *know* she isn't."

***

There were no more rallies until the Easter holidays, and as if Sandy knew she was in danger of being got rid of, she behaved quite well out on their rides now. She still found leaves fluttering in the wood or a bird in the hedge very frightening, but she seemed to spook more slowly, and Clare even found herself laughing when she did it now. Mum's two toes mended, and she rode Sandy a few times, and had to admit she was comfy. Dad had agreed to give Sandy another chance and everything was going along quite nicely…until the Riding and Road Safety Test. In the Pony Club you can take various tests to show that your riding is improving, and Clare and her friends were all hoping to take the C test at camp this summer. This is the third test you take and you can't try for it unless you have passed your Riding and Road Safety Test, to show you're safe to ride alone on the road.

The Riding and Road Safety Test should have been a doddle for Clare, as Sandy was so good in traffic. She and Mum were quite confident as the trailer turned into the college grounds where the test was being run. They had ridden along that road fairly often and Sandy had always been perfectly well behaved. But – and it was a big but in Sandy's case – the first part of the test was in a field on a 'pretend' road. There were pretend crossroads, with painted white lines on the grass, and mock traffic lights, and even chairs and tables in pretend gardens by the side of the pretend road.

It was all too much for Sandy. She spooked, ran backwards, then charged past everything, at what felt like ninety miles an hour, straight over all the white lines, nearly knocking over one set of traffic lights. "Well, bless my soul," said one of the older stewards as he leapt out of the way of a flying plastic bollard. "Where does she think she is? Brands Hatch?" "Poor Sandy," Clare wailed as Mum rushed to catch hold of her bridle. "Of course she doesn't like all this! I've never seen traffic lights in a field either!"

They went off to a quiet corner and the pony soon settled down, but when they had to go back near the hazards for the second part of the test, she snuffed and snorted, and went into her mega-trot until she was out of sight of it all.

Clare sat the written part of the test, although something told her it was a waste of time. 'Never mind,' she consoled herself. 'At least when we get out on the *real* road, they'll all see how good she is in traffic.' She handed in her paper and went to get saddled up again.

Poor Clare! This just wasn't her day. Sandy was really nappy on the way down to the main gate. Clare got more and more tense as she tried to make her go forward and then – you guessed it – Sandy stopped in the gateway and refused to budge. It was one of her classic 'planting' jobs.

Clare's kicking and squeezing had no effect at all and she simply refused to go out on the road. Clare turned her head in misery. On one side she saw Mum trying to decide on the most encouraging expression to have on her face. On the other side, a short way down the road, next to the police examiner, there was an official steward. Oh *NO*! It was Mrs Franks. Clare saw her stare at Sandy, then turn to the policeman and speak to him. They both wrote something down on their clipboards. Mum came running over. "Come on darling, this is pointless. Let's go home, you can take it again in September." She nearly said "...on another pony that won't be so mean to you," but stopped when she saw Clare's face.

Sandy went straight into the trailer, of course, as she always did on these occasions, and they set off home. Clare was mortified. "Sandy didn't get a chance to show them how brilliant she is on the road. They don't understand how she felt." A tear slid out of the corner of her eye and she sniffed. "It's not fair!" Just to rub salt into her wounds, Clare's three best riding friends all passed with flying colours, so at rallies they moved up another ride and started working for their C tests without her. But Clare still loved Sandy, she always had an excuse for her, defended her fiercely when people criticised her, and refused to listen to anyone who suggested that maybe she wasn't the right pony for her.

***

The Easter holidays were over and the nights got longer and the days warmer again. Clare could ride most evenings after school, sometimes with Mum, but mostly on her own. She loved being out on Sandy with nobody there to make remarks or unkind suggestions about her. She didn't see much of her friends either, but just at the moment that was how she liked it. Sandy was her best friend now, whatever they all said!

***

The summer came round, and shows and events started happening in fields and parks, on farms and in woodlands. The roads were crowded with trailers and horseboxes, all sizes and in all states of repair, some with smart ladies in the front, and some crammed with noisy scruffy children and dogs, and sometimes rows of rosettes along the windscreen. Clare longed to win some with Sandy.

She loved getting her ready, making her all clean and shiny. Sandy really enjoyed having a bath. She stretched her neck and curled back her top lip as the water ran across her neck and shoulders. The only precarious moment was washing her back end. If she wasn't expecting the water to come sloshing under her tail, her legs would buckle and she would end up sitting down in the yard. Unless you jumped out of the way fast you could get squashed, or soaked, or both.

"Sandy, what on earth do you think you're doing?" Mum shouted crossly, the first time it happened. On that occasion Dad was passing and, rather unexpectedly, he stuck up for the pony. "Well I don't think I'd much like a bucket of water thrown up my bottom either." He grimaced in horror, and they all laughed. Sandy had recovered her dignity by this time and was calmly pulling at her haynet. She was *so* easy to look after.

Clare overheard Mum say to Dad later that day: "It's a good job she is easy, because she's not much use to Clare when we go out anywhere. Honestly, she's horrid to her sometimes."

Clare couldn't be bothered to go in and argue with them. She just thought to herself, "We'll show them, won't we Sandy? We'll do something good soon. Win a cup, maybe. Then they'll be sorry they were ever mean about you." And she took herself off to bed, to dream of clear rounds and rosettes. One day well behaved – the next day, not. That was Sandy. And she always seemed to have a bad day when there was something happening, like a rally or a show. If she was fairly good in a lesson then she seemed to delight in attracting a crowd by refusing to go in the trailer afterwards. And if she loaded sweetly, she'd usually caused a rumpus of some kind earlier in the day.

For instance she decided that the orange tape around the ring at one show was deadly to horses, and that she couldn't possibly go near it. At another show, the loudspeakers were playing up, and I don't have to tell you who was in the middle of a round of jumping when they started squawking and then went off in a series of loud bangs! Sandy bolted round the ring, and nothing would persuade her to go back, even when things were quiet again. Clare tried so hard not to mind, but she was miserable and tense, and that just made Sandy worse. In showing classes she would fall asleep in the line, and then Clare couldn't get her going again when it was their turn in front of the judge. As for doing Handy Pony, I'm afraid Sandy wasn't handy at all.

Poor Clare, her face was almost permanently red in Pony Club circles. Twice Dad had spoken to her about getting another pony and twice the conversation had ended in tears.

Even Jack, who usually kept well out of ponies, tried to talk to her. "If we've got a loser on our team, we get rid of him," he said helpfully. "There's no point in going on and on with someone who's never going to be any good." Clare jumped on him and started to pummel him and Dad pulled them apart. But this time he seemed to be more cross with Jack than with her. 'Parents,' she thought, 'I'll never understand them.' One thing Mum and Dad were definite about: when Clare's money ran out, they were not going to support a pony who was "mean and ungenerous". She'd never yet gone clear over a jump course, and although she'd finally got a fourth rosette at a Mountain and Moorland show, there were only four in the class! However, much she stood up for Sandy, Clare knew that people felt she was mad to go on with her. Even worse, she began to realise they felt sorry for her. Clare had worked out that Gran's money would just about last until Pony Club Camp. Sandy would have to be shod two weeks before then, and that would take the last of it – she'd already got her feed put by. And so, as she looked over the fence at Sandy grazing, she crossed her fingers and made a wish. She was so lovely, with her summer coat flecked with grey, and her black mane and tail gleaming. "Be good at camp Sandy," she wished. "Be good to me, so we can do well, get placed in the event, and then they'll let me keep you." Sandy, oblivious to the threat hanging over her, just went on munching.

***

If you've been to Senior Camp you'll know what a worry it is just getting there. It means a week away from home often with your pony in a barn with stalls, and only the Pony Club stable boss to advise and help you. You have to take everything you need for the whole time. If you forget something crucial, you may get a chance to send a message home, but probably your family can only visit on the last two days to see you competing in the dressage, show jumping and cross-country. You're most likely to be in a tent or a makeshift dormitory with several other people, and you don't get much sleep. You don't get much of a wash, either. So you need several changes of clothes! You'll be part of a team for the week, and all your horse skills are given marks out of ten, then added up and the best team wins a cup. Riding, tack and turn out, sleeping quarters, and, of course, stable management – everything is inspected and everything has to be correct. It's very hard work and the pressure is on most of the time, in fact it can be murder! But then there are the things you learn, the things you achieve, the things you never realised you could do. There are also the midnight feasts, with spine tingling ghost stories, the barbecues, quizzes, the fancy dress – and the water fights! It's serious and hectic, but also exciting, and fun, with tears and spills and thrills all mixed up together. But the main thing is you can really get to know your pony and form a partnership with them that can sometimes last throughout both your lives. And that is what Clare was counting on.

Sandy had picked up the tension at home, and, of course, she wouldn't load. Even Mum was nearly in tears by the time the pony suddenly relented and trundled up the ramp. By the time they arrived, most of the others were already in their stalls, some on shavings, some on straw. The girl in charge of the stabling turned away from a pretty chestnut, saw Clare leading Sandy along the barn, and stared in horror: 'Good grief, who on earth is this?' she said to herself.

Clare gave her name and the girl clicked her tongue in irritation. "Well, she's very large. Nobody told me about that. I'll have to put her in the end. I hope she'll fit into a stall. She doesn't kick does she? I hope not, with those feet."

They had a bit of a tussle getting Sandy to agree to being in such a confined space, but once a haynet appeared she quickly settled and tucked in. Feeling much relieved, Clare looked along the barn at the tall thin girl who was to be Sandy's boss for the week. She was explaining in a loud voice about the importance of "strict discipline in a barn full of horses".

A boy of about fourteen muttered, "I would have thought that was obvious!" and another boy sniggered. "Who is she?" Clare asked. "Did she do Junior Camp?"

Becky, who owned the pretty chestnut, said: "No, apparently her mother said she ought to put something back into Pony Club, as she got so much out of it when she was our age." She pulled a face "I hope my mum doesn't get any ideas like that! I'd hate it!" "She thinks she knows it all," the boy said, as he chucked his pony's droppings into a bucket. 'She probably does', Clare thought miserably, and she tried to brush all Sandy's shavings back into her stall. "Keep all this middle part clear please at all times." The thin girl spoke as if her word was law. "I don't want a wisp of straw or one shaving out of place. Inspections will be done two or three times a day, with no warning, so keep on your toes. Have they all got hay? What on earth sort of knot is that supposed to be, Susan? Don't you know anything? If that net came loose your horse could get caught in it and break its leg. That's two marks off tonight's score and your pony's hardly settled in. Not a very good start!" Susan rubbed her nose vigorously and struggled with her haynet. "I hate Melanie Franks," said someone else as they walked to their tents.

Clare stopped dead in horror. No wonder she'd seemed familiar. Melanie Franks, that horrid woman's daughter. Oh no, this was going to be the longest week of her life. 'Sandy,' she thought. 'Please behave. Please, please – behave!"

***

I need hardly tell you that Sandy didn't. Clare tried so hard not to let down her team, but the more she tried the worse Sandy was. She started in the second ride, but was moved down when Sandy kept napping and stopping and holding the others up. The dressage was a nightmare. She went round with her nose poked out, all her weight on her forehand and swinging her bottom out instead of bending. Several times she wandered out of the arena altogether. Clare might as well not have been there at all, for all the notice Sandy took of her. Her riding marks were poor, of course, and though she tried not to mind and the others tried to be kind, it just got harder as the week went on. As far as Melanie Franks was concerned, this was one of the worst ponies she'd encountered. Sandy quickly got the knack of undoing her bar and getting out of her stall, wandering up the barn and rummaging round the feed bins, eating anything left in the buckets. She'd wind up all the other ponies, until the noise they made brought Melanie storming over to Clare's tent to haul her back to the barn.

"Just sort your wretched elephant out," she growled. "I've had enough of it!" Clare began to think Melanie was worse than her mother. She'd tried to make an escape-proof stall with extra bars and extra baler twine, so Sandy then mastered the art of sticking her head through her window, twisting her neck and extending her lips to eat the haynet of the pony next door. This was a docile grey who was far too timid to stand up to the Incredible Hulk beside her. Sandy threatened to bite her if she tried. Then she managed to get out of the stall again, by simply leaning back on the bars until they gave way, then she wandered about where she liked. On the fourth day Melanie requested that Sandy be sent home. Clare was beside herself. The DC was consulted. She rang Mum and Dad and only after they explained that Clare was being given "one last chance" to get to grips with Sandy, did the DC consent to her staying: "Against my better judgment," she told them. "And, on one condition." The condition was that she must be separated from the other ponies to leave them in peace. There was only one box available, and whose horse was comfortably ensconced in there? Melanie Franks was not pleased when her smart little Arab had to move into Sandy's stall. As you can imagine this was almost the last straw, and Clare's stable marks hit rock bottom. By now the rest of the green team were hardly speaking to her and Clare went off her food and couldn't sleep. Her friends tried to cheer her up, but they all knew that Sandy was going to be sold, and secretly they thought it was about time. So they really didn't know what to say to her. It was much easier to avoid her whenever they could. Clare *would* have longed for camp to be over, except for one thing. Going home brought nearer the day that Sandy would have to go.

Things could hardly have been worse, but still she loved that pony.

***

On the last but one day she woke to a grey dismal sky. 'The weather looks just like I feel,' she thought, as she mucked out Sandy's stable and cleaned her tack. She really didn't want to be with anyone else, so she stayed with her pony and didn't go for breakfast.

The dressage instructor had to come looking for her when it was time to take her test. Clare was in the box with her arms round Sandy's neck. "Come on Clare, never say die," the dressage lady said with as much optimism as she could manage.

Clare was too tired to argue, but she knew it was all a bit pointless.

"You never know, she might suddenly get the idea," the dressage lady continued. She knew, like everyone else, that this pony was going to be sold. She watched Clare as she rode down to the arena. Nice girl, pity about the pony. In the distance Clare spotted Declan making encouraging faces at her. Then without any warning the dark clouds broke open, the rain bucketed down, and everyone got soaked. Clare just laughed: it was so typical of her luck at the moment.

Sandy went round rather better than anyone expected, and Declan said to her as she came out: "You see, you can show 'em if you really want to."

She hoped he couldn't see she'd been crying. "Your Dad and

Mum are coming for the cross-country this afternoon," he added. "I saw them just now heading for the pub." As Clare went to give Sandy her lunch the wind was so fierce it was blowing the chaff out of the bucket. A flash of lightning startled them both, and then the thunder crashed right overhead. Clare nearly jumped out of her skin, but Sandy ignored the noise and went on calmly scoffing her feed. The rain slowly eased off and the storm passed over, and they inspected the course and decided it was safe to go on with the competition. It was a bit slippery in places, and one of the drop fences was taken out.

Clare was drawn to go towards the end, so she had time to talk to Mum and Dad before warming Sandy up. And that was a mistake. "This is the end of it Clare," Dad said before Mum could stop him. "She's going – you must see it's a waste of time. Find something smaller and kinder, and get rid of her." "Oh Clare, come back," Mum cried. "Now look what you've done." she turned on her husband and glared. "Poor girl. You could have waited 'til we got them home." But in her heart, Mum agreed with him.

***

Clare put the tack on and rode to the furthest corner of the warm-up area. Tears were streaming down her face now. Sandy trotted quietly round puzzled by the feeling she got from her rider. When her number was called Clare felt numb. She didn't care what happened. The rain began to fall again and it hid her tears. Sandy took the first few easy fences in her stride. There was another rider in front and she just followed him. Then that horse stopped, and so did Sandy, at a little log pile with a ditch in front.

And the jump judge?

It was Mrs Franks. Sandy had the inevitable three refusals and Mrs Franks eliminated her. "You can carry on, but don't hinder anyone else," she shouted from her car. She didn't bother to look up to see who it was wearing number 27. She just crossed her off on the sheet and wrote a big E in the margin. The rain was bucketing down now and the sky was black again. Jill Johnson, the DC, appeared in her Land Rover. Clare couldn't face her, or the thought of Mum and Dad waiting out on the course, and she dug her heels into Sandy's side and turned her off across the heath. The Land Rover suddenly swerved towards them in the mud and caught its wheels on a small tree stump. It snapped and flicked towards Sandy who rolled her eyes and bolted. Clare still didn't care. She clung on and started to laugh. Sandy might as well go out with a bang, she thought, as she careered past a bunch of soggy riders who were going back to camp to get out of the rain. "Oh no, it's Clare…Oh that pony…Poor Clare." The voices faded as she disappeared into the woodland on the edge of the course. Sandy was good at taking care of herself. She was very sure-footed, so she hardly slackened her pace even though there was not much room for error among the branches. Then they saw the fallen tree. It was right across the path and it was big. The ground was like a skating rink here, and they slipped and slithered towards it. Clare let out a shriek. It looked huge when they got right up to it, but before either of them had time to think, Sandy threw herself upwards and cleared it by a mile. Then she shied violently at something strange on the other side.

Something was caught under the smaller branches. Oh no – not some thing – somebody! Clare hauled on the reins and Sandy skidded round. Clare jumped off and ran over. It was a girl. There was no sign of a horse, and the girl wasn't in cross-country colours. She had her head on one side and her legs were trapped just below the knees. Clare knelt down beside her. The hat was slightly askew, and Clare craned her neck to look at the girl's face. It was Melanie Franks. That huge crash of thunder she'd heard just now! The lightning must have split this tree as Melanie was riding under it. If only she'd got her mobile! She looked round frantically, to see Sandy standing quietly behind her, eating the grass, as usual. Clare tried to move the branch that was trapping Melanie – but it was impossible. She pulled off her cross-country top and laid it over the older girl's back. She knew she mustn't move her and she knew she must get help – and quickly. Melanie was pale and a bit cold but she was breathing. Clare pulled the numnah from under the saddle and put that over Melanie too. And then she clambered on and turned Sandy round. But where were they? She'd lost her bearings with the rain and the wind, and now she could hear nothing to guide her. And this huge tree – she must get back over. There was no other way through the tangle of bushes and brambles.

She turned Sandy round, gritted her teeth, closed her eyes and charged. Sandy flew it again, as if she knew she had to, and shot back through the wood. Because she had no idea where to go, Clare dropped the reins and Sandy found her own way. As they reached open ground she turned to the right without any signal from her rider, and they were cantering fast towards camp when the DC's Land Rover appeared. Mum and Dad and Mrs Franks were all crammed in with her. The girls had told them about Sandy bolting, and then Melanie's Arab had appeared, on her own with the stirrups flapping, so they'd all set off in pursuit. Clare blurted out the news, and they followed Sandy back into the wood. Mrs Franks was the first to reach her daughter and wrap her gently in a blanket. The DC got straight onto her mobile, and within a short time, firemen and medics lifted Melanie clear and she was on her way to hospital. Only then would Clare return to camp with Sandy. They were all soaked through and Clare was shivering with cold now. She was wearing Dad's mac, and Dad and Mum walked beside her. Mum had a hand on the pony's neck, and was absentmindedly stroking her. Nobody said anything about Sandy's future, but when, on the next morning, Clare went into the show jumping ring and did a lovely clear round, Declan came up behind Mum and Dad as they were cheering their daughter.

"I knew they'd get it together," he said. "Clare just had to relax. That's a clever mare that, and once Clare stopped being nervous and worrying if everything was all right, I knew that it would be! This pony'll be fine now, so enjoy her. One good thing – she'll last Clare forever, the size she is!" Clare came out of the ring and rode up to them, beaming. Sandy seemed to be rather pleased with life, too. Mrs B.O. came past with a tray of tea for the stewards.

"Ah," she said. "The heroine. I told you that mare could jump. It's lucky for Melanie she can." She neatly rescued a packet of biscuits, just as Sandy was about to demolish them,

"Well done Clare. And I'm glad to see a smile at last. I was beginning to think it was my cooking." Clare laughed, took up her reins and cantered off up the slope to where some of her friends were waiting. As Sandy's large rear end was disappearing, Declan said in his most Irish voice: "Ah, well now, there is just one thing. As a favour to me, and to preserve me reputation as a serious dressage instructor, could you ever find a way to persuade Clare to keep that fat backside out of my lessons?" He threw back his head and laughed, and Mum and Dad joined in. Clare stood up in her stirrups and looked back at them. People had always laughed at Sandy, and at Clare for loving her, but something told her now that it was Sandy who'd had the last laugh after all.

The Shetland

The Shetland

"Can I, Mum, can I? Please? They said at the stables today there are lots needing homes, or even just on loan. If I work really hard and save all my money, do you think I can have a pony of my own? I'll look after it all by myself, I will, honestly!"

Mum clattered the dishes onto the draining board and made a grumpy noise. Not all this again.

"I don't want to talk about it any more, Laura." She tried to smile as she spoke, but the look in her eye told Laura, "Don't push it." So Laura didn't. She went up to her room and peeled off her jodhpurs. She climbed into some dilapidated dungarees, washed her hands, and went out into the tiny garden. Mum looked out of the kitchen window and saw her lying on the grass, devouring every word of the latest *Pony* magazine. "We can't do it – we've not got the cash!" Mum sighed to herself. She squeezed out the washing up sponge and left it to dry. Laura was nine and pony mad. Small for her age, but clever and strong, she could fill all the water buckets at the stables on her own and hardly be out of breath. She spent all the weekends there and most evenings too, mucking out and cleaning tack. In exchange she got two free rides a week. "She's as happy as Larry down there," Dad kept saying. "She never wants to come home! Maybe we *should* try and get her a pony."

"What with?" Mum retorted. "And anyway, where could we keep it?"

Whenever Mum said that, Laura always wanted to say, "At

the stables, of course!" but she knew that cost money, and things were tight since her Dad had been made redundant last year.

She also suspected that Mum didn't like her spending all her time with ponies, and there Laura was right. Mum secretly longed for what she thought of as 'a real little girl' who liked girly clothes, and dancing, and music. Especially music. Mum loved music. She still had the old upright piano that she'd learnt on as a girl, and sometimes in her daydreams she imagined her daughter playing at the Royal Albert Hall, in a long floaty dress with a huge orchestra behind her.

Laura was blissfully unaware of these fantasies. Laura just wanted to be with horses. So Mum and Laura had an agreement. It was Dad's idea, and Laura had to admit it was fair. As long as she went to piano lessons once a week, and promised to practise at least every other day then she could go to the stables the rest of the time.

And Laura kept to this agreement, because all she really wanted to do was ride...and one day to have a pony of her own. She was saving all her pocket money, and Christmas money. She'd got £27 in a box under her bed. The box had a gorgeous grey Highland pony on the lid and other ponies all round the sides. Laura was certain of one thing. She *would* get her own pony one day, and so she went on reading every horsey book that she could find, riding round the school twice a week, mucking out, cleaning tack...and saving. She didn't mind what sort of pony she got. It didn't have to be smart or showy. It only had to have four legs, a head and a tail. She wouldn't even mind if it didn't have a tail! A scruffy cross-breed would do, or a little Welsh pony, or a Shetland. A Shetland! Now that was a good idea. They probably didn't cost so much to buy. Some people said they were mean and naughty, but Laura knew that most ponies were what people made them. That's what they said about dogs, and children, too. She wondered what her parents were making of her?

***

When she'd read every word of her magazine, Laura hauled herself up and went in to the piano. She was working for her Grade Three. The pieces were quite hard, and there were lots more scales this time. The exam was just before her birthday and she needed to pass to keep Mum happy. She lifted the lid and flexed her fingers determinedly.

***

Four years earlier – before Laura had even sat on a pony – a good-natured bay Shetland mare called Morag had given birth on a distant farm in Cumbria. It was very early in the morning. The last stars were just fading from the April sky and it was an easy birth. Morag had done it several times before, and she calmly licked her foal's nose and face and waited for her to stagger to her feet and grope for some milk. Around her some other mares had foals at foot, and some were still waiting. They moved heavily about as they searched for the shoots of spring grass. Morag's foal was named Woodhurst Millie and she grew into a pretty bay yearling. She was darker than her mother with a rather fetching mealy-coloured nose, almost like an Exmoor, and huge dark eyes. She would probably make 38 inches high and was nicely put together, with neat round feet. The only thing that let her down was her skin, especially under her mane and tale, and as she grew it became clear that she suffered from sweet itch. A sweet itch pony's skin is extra sensitive. It gets irritated by the flies and midges, especially in the early mornings and evenings, and this makes the pony rub and rub until it's sore and miserable.

As there were so many other ponies and foals to look after, Millie's sweet itch got neglected and she was a sorry sight by the time she was two. Several people came to buy Shetlands, but nobody fancied the one with the bald tail and straggly wisps of mane. So Millie got moved around the stud, ending up as nursemaid for the newly weaned foals. The people at the stud didn't want to put her in foal in case the baby had sweet itch too. She began to be ignored by the grooms. They just threw her some hay and broke the ice on her water in winter and left her to it. Someone even muttered, "What's the point in keeping old baldy going? She'll never do anything, with her skin."

Luckily Millie didn't know what they said, but she did rather long for someone to come and talk to her, and make a fuss of her as they'd done when she'd been small. She liked people, and she was bored standing about doing nothing. Nothing, that is, except when she scratched and scratched, trying to get relief from the itching. She was there as usual by the fence, head hanging, looking much older than her four years, when a small group of people appeared in the next paddock.

***

In another part of England lived an actress called Sylvia Graham. She loved horses. She'd always loved horses, and when she was a child in Somerset she'd had several ponies of her own. As she got older she was in all the Pony Club teams, and was beginning to think about riding as a career, when she was offered a small part in a film about horses, and was "discovered". Now, fifteen years on, she was a successful actress with several smart TV credits to her name. And she was happily married, with a young daughter, Gwen.

Because Sylvia was so often away from home working, Gwen got rather spoiled. One Christmas, she was watching TV, and saw the Shetland Pony Grand National at Olympia. She watched the ponies tearing round the arena and flying over the brush fences, and she squealed with excitement. She heard the cheers and clapping from the packed audience and called Sylvia in to watch. "Oo Mummy I want to do that," she said, bouncing up and down in the chair. "Please Mummy, can I?"

Immediately after the Christmas break, Sylvia set out to find a pony for her, and one of her old riding friends gave her the phone number of a smart Shetland stud in Cumbria. Yes, you've guessed. It was Sylvia in the paddock next to Millie's that day. She was looking at a palomino gelding with a flaxen mane and tail, deliciously hairy, tossing his head as if he knew his mane was his crowning glory.

"He's just five," the owner was saying. "He's been backed, and he's going nicely. He's well up to height and I think he's what you're looking for. He was going to Holland but the sale's just fallen through. You're lucky, ponies like this one don't come on the market very often." "Oo Mummy, I must have him," said Gwen, fluttering her eyelashes and pouting in the way her mother found irresistible. Sylvia looked him over carefully. She felt his legs and picked up his feet. As she turned and straightened up, a dark shape caught her eye. "Oh dear, someone looks a bit sad," she said. The stud owner felt rather annoyed. Someone should have moved Millie. They knew Miss Graham was coming today. Really, it was too careless of them. That pony let down the whole stud down, poor creature. Sylvia moved towards the fence, and he followed her hastily. "Aw she's a kind pony, quite well put together," he muttered. "Such a shame about the sweet itch." Sylvia Graham felt a wave of sympathy sweep over her. As a child she'd had a pony called Smarty with the same problem, and a friend of hers had concocted a lotion from nettles and other herbs that had really helped him. Childhood memories flooded in, and before she knew what she was doing she heard herself saying, "Well, if you can accept a sensible price, I'll take her as well. I'm going to keep him in livery near me, and she'll be company for him."

* * *

Laura slung her bike up against the fence. She was late. Mum had made her play all her scales again, even though she'd done them twice on Wednesday! Laura hated scales, especially on stable days. She dashed into the feed room, and stopped short in the doorway. Two spotless stainless steel bowls stood gleaming amongst the dilapidated plastic buckets. The bowls each contained a small exotic-looking feed and some crisp sliced apples. "Who are these for?" she asked.

Sally the head stable girl, said, "New arrivals. Two Shetlands down from Cumbria. One's a beauty, not sure why they got the other one – she's bald." Sally was from Cardiff. She'd been at the stables for three years, but, as she was always proclaiming in her lilting accent, she still hadn't got the hang of the English: "Where I come from people aren't afraid to show their feelings!" She was a big kind girl, and she had a very soft spot for this small person, who biked here in all weathers, and did any job you asked her to, just to be amongst the horses. Something flickered in Laura's heart as she looked over the door at Millie. Bald she might be, but those eyes! The pony whickered gently and stood patiently until Laura placed the feed in front of her. Putting one hand on the pony's shoulder, Laura watched the skin twitch under her fingers. "What's her name?" she called as Sally passed the door.

"Millie," Sally replied. "Lorenzo's gorgeous – come and see."

He certainly was, his coat gleaming and mane bouncing as he guzzled his food. But Laura went back and looked again at Millie. The pony lifted her head and whickered again.

"What do you want, someone to make a fuss of you, too?" Laura knelt beside her and felt a soft mealy nose pressed into her neck. That was it. She was lost. Bowled over. Hopelessly in love.

After stables she dashed home to her shelf crammed with horse books, and looked up sweet itch. She didn't understand some of the long words, but she knew it was a common problem and was sure Millie had it. And she was going to cure her. Next day, she raided her savings tin and went to their local tack shop. There she bought a rather expensive bottle of white lotion. As she biked into the yard later, she passed a large powder-blue car in the gateway. From Lorenzo's box came the sound of voices. "Urgh, I don't want to ride that thing too," a child's voice whined. "She's tatty and awful." "Well, she must have some exercise and she can't go out into the field because of the flies," said a woman. "If I was lighter I'd ride her myself. Sally, have you someone who could take her out for me?"

Laura heard Sally laugh, and say: "We've got just the rider for you Miss Graham, and I'm not sure, but I *might* be able to persuade her!" She laughed again.

Laura moved quickly out of sight as they came back into the yard. She peeped through a gap in the door at Gwen Graham. She was a little taller than Laura, with long blonde hair and a button nose. She was immaculate in stretch jodhpurs and sparkling new boots. Sylvia looked laid back and elegant in something that probably cost a fortune. But Laura hardly saw them at all. Her mind was running away with her. Did Sally mean her to be that rider? Laura was sure she did. Usually with the ponies in full livery, only one rider did all the exercising, unless the owners rode them too. If this Gwen girl didn't like Millie, then maybe she could be the only one to ride her? She could pretend she was hers!

Laura dashed through her chores, and as she was polishing the last stirrup leather she heard the sound of small hooves in the yard. She looked out of the tackroom and saw Lorenzo, resplendent in new saddle and bridle, and Gwen about to get on. Then Sally led Millie out of her box and winked at Laura. Sylvia Graham came over to her, and smiled somewhat doubtfully.

"Do you think you could just sit on for me while we go out for a look round?" she asked Laura. "I don't know how she'll behave, she's not been ridden much – so I'd better walk with you. We won't go far this first time." Laura needed no second bidding. She rinsed her hands under the tap, grabbed her crash hat and took hold of Millie's reins. Once on, she sat as still as she could, trying not to irritate her withers or her neck. Millie tensed up and moved gingerly forward. "It's all right, Mills," Laura whispered. "You go as slow or as fast as you like. I won't touch you." Lorenzo led the way out of the yard, across the road, and turned onto the bridlepath that led to the village. Sylvia walked alongside them, ready to grab the reins if either pony started playing up. Millie started to relax a little as she followed the bouncy palomino. Someone seeing the two ponies for the first time might have thought, 'What a strange pair! One pony strutting and gleaming in the sunlight, and one brown lump, trailing along behind.' Laura didn't care what anyone thought. She was in seventh heaven, and to her the brown lump was the most precious pony she'd ever sat on. After ten minutes or so they turned for home and Sylvia said, "Let's try a gentle trot darling...oh and you too, Lara, could you manage that?" Laura bit her tongue and nodded. She was tempted to say, "much better than Gwen by the look of her", but she realised she mustn't upset things now or she might not get to ride Millie again. As they trotted, Millie began to lengthen her stride and she soon caught up with Lorenzo. Sylvia was left behind, and Gwen glared at Laura.

"Please keep that tatty thing away from my pony," she said. "He might catch something horrid, so don't let her near me – or can't you stop?" She smirked, and Laura flushed scarlet and slowed Millie to a walk. "I don't know why Mummy got her," Gwen went on. "I don't want her, she's no use to anyone. My Lorenzo's going to do the Shetland Grand National in London at Christmas. Mummy says he'll easily qualify for Olympia, and if he doesn't she'll get me another one who will." And with that she pushed past Laura and rode back to her mother.

Millie was hot and tired when Laura untacked her. "I'll bet you haven't been ridden for ages." Laura whispered in her ear. "I bet you've just been ignored. Well I think you're lovely, and who wants to go to stupid old Olympia anyway." As Laura brushed her head, Millie nudged her gently and gazed at her with liquid brown eyes.

* * *

Millie had been broken in as a three year old, but not ridden much because of her skin, so wearing tack every day gave her a few problems. To make her feel more comfortable, Laura started putting an old tea towel under the smart felt pad Sylvia had bought. It must be marvellous to have enough money to buy anything you wanted, she thought, as she buckled the girth and pulled it tight. Yet money didn't seem to make Gwen very happy. She never came to see Lorenzo except to ride him, and more often than not one of the other girls got him ready for her, and turned him out afterwards.

Laura thought to herself: 'They'll never get to know each other like that.' She, of course, did everything for Millie. She put on the white lotion twice a day, and washed her mane and tail with special soap every weekend. Gradually the split wrinkled skin was beginning to look more normal and her twitching began to subside. Millie was what Sally called "a very chatty pony". She talked to Laura all the time, calling as soon as she heard her voice in the yard, and making little conversational noises as they got ready to go out. And on a ride the brown lump was transformed! Her head came up, she pricked her ears, pointed her toes and really showed herself off. Laura thought she was absolutely beautiful. Usually Millie and Lorenzo went out together, and although Gwen was a neat competent rider, she spent most of the time talking about clothes, and pop music and the telly. She said she wanted to be an actress when she grew up, and was always boasting about how many famous people she knew.

Laura, by contrast, said very little. She didn't care who'd been round to Gwen's house for supper, or what they'd said to her about her recitations and songs. Actually Laura could think of nothing worse than having to listen to those! So she just kept quiet, and worked at keeping Millie collected and steady when they trotted and cantered. She felt more at home on the pony with every outing. One day they came across some logs, newly felled in the wood. "Let's have a jump," Gwen said. "He's ready now, and I must get him going so we can qualify this year. You go first while I check his girth. Go on, what are you waiting for? Not chicken, are you?" She bent down to pull the strap up a hole, and Laura put her tongue out at her back. She turned Millie, and took her to look at the log pile. Then she cantered up to it, and Millie pricked her ears and popped over it as if she'd been jumping for years. Lorenzo was just the opposite, napping to the side, and then running out. Gwen tried three or four times, but

he refused to go near the logs. "Shall Millie and me give you a lead?" Laura asked. She knew this would make Gwen furious, but she couldn't resist the chance to get her own back. Sure enough, Gwen lost her temper and hit Lorenzo several times, whereupon he whipped round, dropped his shoulder, and threw her into some nettles.

Laura put her hand to her mouth to hide a grin, then trotted after Lorenzo, and got off Millie to catch him.

"I know what," said Gwen. "Let *me* ride *her*. If she jumps like that, maybe I should swap and get rid of him."

She jumped onto Millie and snatched up the reins. Laura could see the pony wasn't happy, and winced as Gwen jerked her round, dug in her heels and charged towards the logs. Millie sailed over them, jumping so big that Gwen got left behind and jagged the pony in the mouth.

"Don't ride Millie like that!" The words were out before Laura could stop them. "You'll hurt her, she's got a very soft mouth."

Gwen stared down at this upstart. "She's my pony, not yours," she snapped. "And don't you forget it. Just stand there and hold Lorenzo and shut up." She jumped the logs several more times, hauling Millie round afterwards instead of giving her time to turn comfortably, and then making her jump straight back again. Millie put up with this for a while, but then she'd had enough, and suddenly stopped. Gwen shot up her neck, only just staying on, and banged her cheek on Millie's head. She heaved herself back and then hit Millie hard across her withers. The pony flinched in pain and her eyes rolled. Gwen raised her stick again, but Laura grabbed her arm, and pulled her off onto the path.

"Don't you dare hit her again, you horrid, horrid girl!"

Gwen was so surprised she just stood with her mouth open. Laura handed over Lorenzo's reins, vaulted lightly onto Millie and rode away.

Back in Millie's box, panic set in. What had she done? What would happen now? Sylvia Graham doted on her daughter, and she'd believe Gwen instead of her every time. Oh if only she hadn't pulled Gwen off. If only she'd kept quiet. If only...If only...But she couldn't keep quiet – not when Millie was being hurt.

***

"That girl Lara's not to ride my pony ever again," Gwen wailed. "She's a rotten rider, and she's horrid! I'm going to tell Sally to sack her! She doesn't know anything about ponies or jumping or anything, and I hate her!" "All right darling calm down," Sylvia murmured comfortingly. "Leave Lorenzo, they'll see to him. We'll go and get Dr Hughes to look at your poor face. Don't worry darling, I won't let this happen again. Sally will sort her out for us." Laura had hidden behind the feed barn when she saw Gwen riding back in, and she stayed there until she heard the blue car driving away. Then she went back to Millie's box and began washing her mane and tail. She spent ages gently rubbing in the lotion and then brushing and combing the hair until it was dry and free from tangles. Sally looked over the door at the small girl working away on the beloved pony. "Well now," she said, in a serious voice. "What's been going on in the woods today? And I'm not talking about Teddy Bears!"

Laura didn't answer. She kept her head bent and went on picking out Millie's foot, even though there was not a speck of mud left in it. "Sylvia's not very pleased with you, I'm afraid," Sally continued. "It seems you were a bit rough with her darling daughter."

"I wasn't!" Laura had to defend herself now. "She's a rotten little fibber if she said I was. She was rough, really rough with Millie...and I...I just made her stop."

She moved round to the other side of the pony, to hide her scarlet cheeks, and pretended to be very busy on Millie's front legs.

Sally moved away, but as she went she said quietly: "It might be better if nothing else nasty happens to Gwen for a while. OK?" On her way home from school the next day Laura bought a card with a kitten on it that said "I'm sorry". She addressed it to 'S and G Graham', biked over before tea, and left it pinned to Lorenzo's door.

***

The following Saturday, Sylvia came and found Laura while she was mucking out. "I don't think you'd better ride with Gwen for a while," she said rather sharply. "I know that you love Millie, and only hit Gwen because you were worried about the pony. But it wasn't a very nice way to behave really, was it? Gwen hurt her face quite badly when you knocked her over, and both the ponies might have run off and caused an accident, after you let go of them. That was silly too wasn't it?"

Laura's cheeks burned. Just as she'd feared, Gwen had completely changed the story to suit herself and make Laura the 'baddie'. Gwen had said she'd hit her! She couldn't think of anything to say, and then to her horror she felt tears of indignation come into her eyes.

Sylvia spoke to Laura more gently now, "Let's forget about it. I'm grateful that you look after Millie so well. You ride her quite nicely too, but she isn't yours. Don't get too attached to her, she may not be here forever you know."

This was the last thing Laura wanted to be reminded of, and she fled, clutching her muck sack, and as she emptied it out onto the heap, she let the tears flow.

***

After that she managed to avoid Gwen completely for a couple of weeks. One weekend Gwen went off to London anyway, and didn't ride Lorenzo for several days afterwards.

"I had to go to the BBC," she announced to no-one in particular. "Twice – because someone else wanted to see me as well." As Gwen chattered on about her auditions, Sally was sweeping the yard. Perspiration was running down the side of her face, and she wiped it on her sleeve as she muttered to Laura: "She'll be filming in blooming Hollywood next."

"Here, Gwen!" she called, waving the broom in her direction. "Do you want to do something useful before you get to be too big a star?" "Oh I can't," squeaked Gwen, recoiling in horror. "Mummy likes me to keep these best jods spotless. Anyway you're paid to do it aren't you?"

She sauntered off, and Sylvia's driver got out and opened the back door for her. Sally stood leaning on the broom handle for a moment, gazing after the big blue car, then sighed and went on sweeping. Things gradually settled down again, and after a while Lorenzo and Millie did go out together again. Laura managed to keep her mouth shut and just rode along behind. Gwen did enough talking for two anyway. When she wasn't showing off about the Shetland Grand National and how she was going to win, she recited poems in a la-di-dah voice or, even worse, she sang, waving her arms about and frightening the birds. She didn't always turn up to ride Lorenzo, and on those days one of the other girls went out with Laura. Then they did have some fun, racing up the grid of jumps in the woods and galloping over the fields, both ponies going like the wind! Like all the other horses in the yard, Millie had one rest day every week, but the sweet itch meant she couldn't go out to graze with the others, so she just wandered round and round her box waiting for something interesting to happen. Most of all she loved to see Laura coming along with her saddle, and then she scraped at her shavings impatiently until the tack was on. They were in complete harmony these days, and when Laura was riding her, she felt almost as if they were one person – one person, with six legs, and one heart...

***

If you want to have a go at the Shetland Grand National Finals in London, either you or your pony must have done it before. It's a fast and furious event and you need to know what you're doing. If all the ponies and riders were new to it, goodness knows what might happen! Over the spring and summer there are qualifying races in various parts of the country. This gives lots of ponies and children from different places a chance to have a go. Sylvia and Gwen were really keen to get to Olympia that next December – as you can imagine, Gwen never wanted to wait for anything – so Sylvia rang the people at the Cumbrian stud. They regularly sent ponies to race, and it wasn't long before they called back to say they'd found a pony for Gwen to get some experience on. He belonged to a friend of theirs who was based reasonably near the stables, and the woman who owned him just happened to be one of Sylvia's biggest fans. The pony was called Samba, and Gwen would be able to ride him in a qualifying race at a local show. Samba was an old hand, and he'd been to Olympia three times. He wasn't quite so fast these days but he jumped really well. In other words, he was a perfect safe introduction to the Shetland Grand National for Sylvia's little treasure. Sylvia rang Sally to tell her the news just as she was getting Lorenzo ready for his young rider, and Sally tried to sound as delighted as Sylvia obviously was! As she put down the phone, she saw Laura struggling past with a huge haynet for one of the big horses. She muttered to herself: "I hope young madam Gwen appreciates how lucky she is," but she doubted that she did.

***

Everyone at the stables was excited about the county show, and Gwen getting a chance to race there. Sylvia graciously offered a lift in her big blue car to Laura and two of the others to watch her little darling perform.

Sally was invited as well. "Thanks all the same Sylvia," she said. "But someone will have to hold the fort here. You've got all my best girls with you today." She inspected them closely. They were smartly dressed in jodhpurs and sweatshirts with the stable logo on the front. "Well you don't look quite so scruffy as usual!" she admitted grudgingly. "Just make sure you behave yourselves, you lot – and don't spend all your money or I'll have your mams and dads on to me." The girls piled into the back of Sylvia's car. They were happy to be travelling in such style, and they had to try very hard not to laugh when Gwen started talking 'race tactics' in the front with her mother.

"I'll try and jump him off in front," she was saying. "That's where they usually win from, isn't it Mummy? And I'll keep him on the inside to save ground on the bends. If he's as fast as he felt when I tried him the other day, I expect I'll qualify him today, and then Lorenzo later. It would be nice to have two ponies in London at Christmas, wouldn't it?"

Sylvia smiled indulgently. Laura stared out of the window and bit on her lip. Her friend Shelley dug her in the ribs and then crossed her eyes and snorted with held-back laughter. "Are you all right in the back? Sylvia asked anxiously. She didn't want someone being sick on the upholstery. It had only just been cleaned.

"Yes, she's fine," Laura said hastily. "I think she just swallowed a fly, that's all."

"Oh dear, like the old lady in the song," Sylvia laughed, and then was pleased that all three girls seemed so amused by her joke. They drove into the competitor's car park, and Laura and the others stared in amazement. There were so many vehicles. Some of them were small pony trailers and some of them were huge lorries. There were even a few boxes with big tents fastened to them and horses inside the tents, in stalls. Some of them looked as big as Laura's house. And some of them were definitely smarter than her house.

Mrs Webb's horsebox was not smart. It was cream and brown and extremely old. There was room for about four ponies inside – so not very large. It's surprising how many Shetlands you can get in, if you pack them carefully!

Mrs Webb was lunging Samba nearby as Sylvia slid her car into the space that had been specially kept for her. He was trotting round very sweetly with his ears pricked. She called over to them: "Just getting the kinks out after the journey."

She was shortish and roundish with curly hair, and when she spoke Laura was surprised by her voice. It was deep and strong, almost like a man's.

"He stiffens up in the trailer these days," Mrs Webb went on. "He's beginning to show his age a bit. Aren't you, old boy?"

As she spoke, as if to deliberately prove her wrong, Samba leapt in the air and started spinning round on the end of the rope. Gwen approached him somewhat cautiously. "Take no notice, Gwen. He's just keen. He loves his racing," Mrs Webb said. "Jump on him, and walk him round. Let him have a look at the bouncy castle and the lawnmower racing. Don't worry, he's seen it all before."

"You can come with me Mummy, if you want," said Gwen, trying not very successfully to sound super-cool. She caught up the reins and clung to them. He hadn't felt like this when she'd practised in Mrs Webb's sand school. Laura and the girls wandered off towards the main rings. A show-jumping competition was going on in the first one they came to, and it had reached the jump-off. They flopped down in a gap between the seating and were cheering for a boy on a cobby grey when an official asked them to move. "You represent a fire hazard," he told them pompously, so they had to get up and stand at the back. They craned their necks to watch the boy, but couldn't see much, so they stumped off to look at something else.

"Let's see what's for sale," said Shelley. "Blow Sally! I must get something to take back for Tigger, even if it's only some mints."

Tigger was a showy little Welsh Section A, and Shelley's favourite.

"Yes, come on," Janet said. She was very quiet and usually just went along with everyone else's plans, but now she set off determinedly towards the tented village.

"Bet she wants to get a lead rope for Star." Star was Sally's own pony, and Janet's favourite. "She's got a bit of a crush on Sally," Shelley whispered to Laura. And, sure enough, they found her choosing a bright blue rope from a huge bunch hanging from a hook like strands of coloured spaghetti. Everything was here – tack, feed, riding clothes. It was an Aladdin's Cave for horse lovers. Laura was just examining a bottle with a label that said 'Herbal Skin Balm – Cures all Complaints, including Sweet Itch' when Mrs Webb came puffing up to her.

"Here you all are," she gasped. "Thank goodness. I've been looking everywhere for you. Samba's just dumped Sylvia's little… er…um…('brat' she was going to say, but thought better of it) and we think her nose is broken. If Samba doesn't race, the last heat will have to be cancelled. There's only three others in it, and they'll be so disappointed." She looked straight at Laura and continued, "Sylvia told me you've been riding one of her other Shetlands for some time. So, will you ride him? I've got lots of crash hats and the silks. What d'you say?" Laura gaped at her. "But. I can't…I…I don't know what to do," she stammered, "Where do we go? And what if I fall off in front of all these people?"

"You won't," Janet said, and Shelley went on excitedly: "You've jumped Millie loads of times over much bigger fences than those, Laura!" Mrs Webb added: "Old Samba knows his way round blindfold. Just sit tight and keep your hands down, and you'll be fine. Come on! Get on and have a quiet canter round. I think you might like him." Both her friends spoke together now:

"Go on Laura!"

"You're heaps better on Shetlands than Gwen ever was anyway."

"Go on!"

"Have a go!" So that was how Laura found herself in the main ring, wearing blue-and-green striped racing colours, and sitting on an elegant grey Shetland. Samba had already decided that he couldn't dislodge this one so easily. Anyway her hands were kind and her seat strong, and he felt like racing now he was in front of all these people. The crowd was cheering and laughing at the sight of these little ponies turned out exactly like thoroughbreds with all the riders in bright racing silks. Laura closed her eyes and tried for a moment to imagine that she had a pair of brown ears flicking in front of her, not grey ones. As she thought of Millie, she felt a surge of confidence go through her body. Samba began to relax under her, and she relaxed too.

They acquitted themselves quite well really, finishing a respectable third, and one or two regular competitors made a note of the small tough child with the light hands, though nobody seemed to know her name or where she came from. Someone said she was with Sylvia Graham, but surely Sylvia's daughter was the blonde girl, the one with that thing on her nose? Mrs Webb was pleased with Laura too, and wrote her name in a little green notebook with a Shetland's head on the front. As for Laura, she couldn't wait to get back to the yard to tell Sally and, of course, Millie, about her wonderful day.

***

"Oh for goodness sake, Laura, no!" said Mum. She was not very happy about this racing thing. It all sounded a bit scary, and what if Laura hurt her hands, or her fingers, with the piano exam coming up? She banged the iron down on to one of Dad's shirts. "Of course you can't do any more racing or 'grand nationalling' – or whatever you call it. You've got your precious Millie to play with round here, as long as Miss Graham needs a rider, and surely that's enough. Now, finish your supper and practise your scales. And then, bed, it's school tomorrow."

Laura stuffed some salad into her mouth and chewed it grumpily. She wished she'd never said anything. Why did grown-ups have to spoil things? Mothers didn't understand about pony things, unless they were 'pony mothers'. She wished she could swap and have Mrs Webb as her mum! Laura got through her practice as fast as she could and went up to her bedroom and shut the door. She got out the guide to the rules of Shetland Racing and studied it carefully. Mrs Webb had also given her a list of all the shows where you could qualify, and she knew more about it all now. It said that only registered ponies could enter. Well, that was all right because Lorenzo and Millie had all their papers. She'd seen them when the vet had done their injections and filled in their passports – something else a pony had to have for Olympia. She took her pyjamas from under her pillow, but instead of changing into them she lay back on the bed and tried to remember every single thing about the day. She relived each thrilling moment. She now had a new aim in life – to ride in London herself one day. She lay trying to sleep but her head was full of wild imaginings. A beautiful dark bay pony with huge eyes was flying over the brush fences. She went round the final turn and up the straight with Laura crouched motionless in the saddle.

"Go on Millie," she was whispering in her ear. "We'll show them."

The commentator's voice was yelling, "They're neck and neck...but now it's Woodhurst Millie...into the lead, Woodhurst Millie going away now...passing the winning post...and it's Woodhurst Millie the winner!!" When Mum looked into the room later, Laura was fast asleep on top of the bed, still wearing her jodhpurs. She was lying on her side, her face buried in the pillow, with one arm above her head in what looked strangely like a victory salute.

***

Gwen now had a grudging respect for Laura though, of course, she still maintained that Samba would have qualified if she'd ridden him. "If only that stupid clown person hadn't spooked him with those juggling things. I was so unlucky!" She turned in her saddle and called, "Let's have a canter. I'll go first, so don't come past me, Laura, will you!"

'At least she's finally got my name right,' Laura thought to herself.

She could put up with Gwen's silliness and boasting now. She just didn't bother to listen any more. And riding Millie made her so happy it was worth putting up with Gwen two or three times a week.

Then came the bombshell. One evening Sylvia Graham turned up on her own and came into the yard to find Sally and Laura scrubbing out the water buckets.

"Oh there you are, Sally," she said. "I'm glad I caught you. We've had a change of plan, just in the last few days. It's rather wonderful news! Gwen's going to be in my new television series. It's a super part for her, more like the lead than mine actually..." she laughed and pulled a face. "She's really more keen on acting than anything else now, so sadly it means Olympia's off. And I'm afraid I'm going to have to give you two weeks' notice with the ponies. This job will be a long-term commitment for us both and we'll have to live in Manchester while we're filming. So, the sensible thing is to sell the Shetlands and maybe get something bigger for her later on. Luckily we've already got an offer for Lorenzo but I don't know about Millie – who'd want to take her on with all her problems... Will you put the word out round here and maybe an advert in *Pony* mag?" She stopped, suddenly aware of two grey-green eyes fixed on her, wide with horror. She opened her mouth to speak again, but Laura had gone. Two weeks' notice! Laura buried her face in Millie's neck. She was too desolate to weep. The soft purr of a motor told her that Sylvia was leaving. Millie shook her head as Laura clung to her. A hand touched her shoulder.

"Now look," Sally's voice said in her ear. "She won't want much for this one, she's too much trouble for most people, what with her skin and everything. How about me talking to your mum?"

Laura nodded miserably. Not that it'd do much good, she thought. Mum just didn't understand. The powder-blue car appeared two days running that week. On the second day, a man and a boy got out and followed Sylvia into Lorenzo's box. Later the boy rode Lorenzo in the school. Laura watched with some satisfaction as he easily cleared the cavalettis, the boy giving with his hands and leaning right up Lorenzo's neck. There was much smiling and handshaking. The next weekend a Land Rover and matching trailer drove off with Lorenzo and all his tack and rugs. Gwen didn't even come to say goodbye to him. Laura rode Millie as usual, but nobody said a word about her future. When the fortnight was nearly up, Laura braved Sally in her little office. "Is there any news about Millie? Selling her I mean?"

Her heart sank to her boots as Sally said, "Sit down a minute Laura."

That's what they said in things on the telly, when there was bad news

"Now Miss Graham's not paying her livery, she can't stay. Anyway Mr Jarvis wants the box. He's got a mare and foal coming for a few weeks."

Mr Jarvis was the owner of the yard. He hardly ever showed his face, just came to check on things occasionally. "And to count the takings!" Sally said.

"I've got some money saved, Mr Jarvis can have that," said Laura desperately. "Who'll look after her? If she goes out and doesn't get her lotion, she'll get bad again, and her mane's just starting to grow back...and she's happy here...and she needs me..." Her voice began to trail off. "Did you speak to my mum...?"

"I'm afraid your mum doesn't feel quite the same as you do Laura." Sally said as gently as she could. Then came the words Laura had been dreading to hear: "Anyway, we may have a buyer for her. Millie's already under offer, so to speak." She went to give her a hug, but Laura was gone.

Laura had decided not to say anything else at home about Millie. She knew that Mum loved her, but she just couldn't understand Laura's passion for ponies. And she knew that Dad would help if he could, but he had problems of his own and she didn't want to make him feel any worse. So she kept her feelings about Millie to herself.

But Mum was worried about Laura. She looked at her anxiously as she played her pieces. She'd been a bit pale for a day or two, and her pillow had felt a bit damp when Mum had made the bed that morning. She hoped Laura wasn't sickening for something. Surely she'd get over this thing about ponies soon? She'd got her exam in two days, and Mum knew she wanted to do well to please her...

***

...But the piano exam was a disaster. It was held in a posh music college, and three people from her school went with one of the mums. As they waited, they sat in a row amongst several older girls. One of them reminded Laura so much of Gwen, with her long blonde hair and posh frock, she felt tears welling up. She had to pinch her nose to stop them. She tried to think of anything except what was happening at the stables, but the longer they waited, the harder it got. Then her name was called. She picked up her music and walked through the double doors.

As she sat down to play at the grand piano, the lovely dark wood suddenly reminded her of the sheen on Millie's neck, and her fingers turned to lead. She tried to play, but her arms wouldn't bend and she sat as if paralysed. "Ahem – I said – D Major." The examiner was feeling a bit peevish. It was almost lunchtime and he'd heard an awful lot of wrong notes that morning. Now he was confronted by what appeared to be a small stone statue in a school uniform. It was too bad. "We really *have not* got all day," he rasped. "Could you please give me the scale of D Major!"

"No, sorry," whispered Laura. She slid off the stool and fled through the door. After school she walked all the way home and then dashed straight up to her room. Mum tried to come in.

"I only want to hear how it all went, darling. Let me in."

"No Mum, please leave me alone. I couldn't play at all. It was hopeless. I'm sorry – just leave me alone."

So, reluctantly, Mum did.

Later Dad came up. He said, "Never mind silly old music exams. You can always take them again."

He put an arm round Laura and hugged her.

Laura looked up at him and stammered, "But Mum will be so disappointed. I...I just couldn't play! And...I'm so sorry Dad."

"Come on Laura, this is not like my girl. Never mind about any of it. Let's think about something jolly, like your birthday treat this weekend." He went on talking about a special cinema trip, and what presents she might get, but after a while she wasn't listening. Millie, Millie – Millie was all she wanted. Going to the stables was almost too painful now, but she knew Millie needed her lotion – June was one of the worst months for flies. So next day after her tea, she biked down there as usual. She turned into the yard and went towards the tackroom to get the bottle, then stopped in horror. There was a large chestnut head sticking out of Millie's box. She dashed to the door, and a fat mare and a gangly foal moved rather nervously away from her. Laura stood and stared at them. They looked so big and clumsy in there. The more she stared the bigger they seemed to grow. They were huge and ugly! She wouldn't have believed she could hate any horse, but she hated these two! Her knuckles were white as she clutched the top of the door with both hands.

As if from nowhere, Sally appeared. "We had to move her out," she said gently. "She's gone. I'm sorry...It'll be a good home Laura, and I'm sure you could go and..." her voice tailed off.

Laura had shot her hands up over her ears. She couldn't believe that Sally had let Millie go without Laura saying goodbye. Not say goodbye to Millie? Her Millie? This wasn't happening, it couldn't be... Suddenly she felt all hot and sticky and then cold and shivery, and then she felt nothing at all as she fell down outside Millie's old stable.

***

The doctor straightened up from the bed. "She needs to rest", he said. "Keep her in bed for twenty four hours, but it's probably just a virus. Bring her in to see me if you're still worried." He smiled at Laura.

'Why does everyone keep smiling?' she thought. 'Don't they know how awful life is?' She turned away as Mum held a cup up to her face. She didn't want to see Mum. She didn't want to see anyone. Nobody loved her. If they did they'd never have let Millie go. All she wanted to do now was sleep, sleep and forget. But when she did sleep her dreams were all of ponies: ponies of every colour, shape and size, but each with huge brown eyes that seemed to look right into her heart. As Laura's temperature dropped next day, she sat up and ate a little. But she felt tired and confused. She couldn't bear to talk to Mum, and Dad didn't seem to be around. She knew Dad understood about Millie, and she wanted him to hold her hand and sit with her. Not to talk – just to be there.

"Where's Dad?" she asked.

"He'll be back later," Mum said briskly and turned her head away. She didn't quite look Laura in the eye and, for the first time, Laura thought of something other than Millie. Mum's face looked all funny. Maybe there *was* something wrong between her and Dad. Oh no, not that as well. She couldn't bear it. From that moment, she decided to make an effort and try and to be much nicer to Mum. There was something wrong. When Dad came in, he barely looked round the door of the sitting-room, where they were watching the TV, and definitely avoided Mum's eyes. Mum didn't say anything. She was still looking a bit odd, and she sat staring at the telly. Then Dad seemed to be out again.

Laura thought, 'If I'd been at home more maybe this wouldn't have happened.' And she felt sad and rather guilty.

Mum made her go to bed early, and she heard Dad come in later on. She went to the loo, and as she crossed back over the landing she stopped. Her parents were talking in the hall.

"What if it all falls through?" Mum was asking in a strained voice.

Dad replied crossly, "I can only do my best, dear. I can't do more. If it doesn't happen, well that's the end of it. Is there anything to eat? I'm starving." "You'll have to do an egg or something," Mum answered wearily. "I'm sorry – I'm too tired." As Mum climbed the stairs, Laura thought she heard the front door close. She ducked back into her room. She lay in bed, her mind going round in miserable circles. Had he gone off out again? Had he and Mum quarrelled? How many times had things fallen through for Dad in this past year? She guessed he was after another job now, and she could tell that he wasn't very hopeful. It was the only time he and Mum fell out – when he was after work. Poor Dad and poor Mum...and...oh dear, she couldn't stop herself thinking it...poor Millie!

***

It was raining the next day – her tenth birthday.

"Just the right sort of day for the pictures," Mum said. Laura sat wearing her new jeans and sweatshirt and gazing out at the grey sky. She wished Mum wouldn't be so jolly. She didn't want to go anywhere, however brilliant the film was supposed to be. Mum had hung up balloons, and they'd sung *Happy Birthday* but Laura didn't think this birthday was going to be much fun.

Dad tooted the horn. "Come on," he shouted, "or we'll miss the beginning!"

Two of Laura's school friends had arrived. They were coming with them to the cinema, and Mum rattled them all out to the car.

As they set off, Dad said: "Oh dear, we're low on petrol, I'll have to double back to the garage."

Mum gave a silly smile in agreement, but Laura's head drooped. That meant passing the stables, and she dreaded it now. They turned into the familiar road and as they did so, she saw someone waving frantically. Dad slowed the car.

"What's up?" he demanded, rather dramatically.

It was Janet, and she managed to gasp out, "Can someone help us a minute? Oh Laura, can you come? There's a pony playing up, and Sally's been knocked down, and there's only me here. The others are out on a ride."

As Laura dashed through the gate, she found herself thinking: 'Good, serves Sally right!' Then she felt awful when she saw Sally flat on her back on the ground. Laura slowed to a walk. Sally was near the muck heap, which looked different. What was it about the muck heap that looked different? The end box seemed nearer to it. And the end box had shrunk. It was only about half the size with a very low door.

"Sally what's happened? Can't you get up?" she called…then stopped as a familiar sound reached her ears. A beautiful familiar sound. She walked towards the new small stable, then stopped and gazed in disbelief. There – standing on a bed of fresh shavings, and wearing a large tartan bow with a label tied to it that said 'Happy Birthday Laura' – was Millie. Nobody said a word, but her friends were clapping and laughing. Laura hugged and hugged the little pony as if she'd squeeze all the breath out of her. Luckily Millie didn't seem to mind. There were a few sniffs and someone blew their nose rather loudly. Laura finally raised her head and gazed at her Mum and Dad. They were standing with their arms round each other. They turned as another figure, with straw in its hair, appeared in the doorway.

The figure spoke: "Thank goodness that's over," said Sally. She seemed to have made a miraculous recovery. "I never want to keep another secret as long as I live. I'm not cut out for it."

"No nor me," said Mum. "I'm hopeless at keeping secrets. But we couldn't tell you until we were sure we could get Millie back. We realised how much she meant to you, and we weren't really sure, even the night before last. Dad said he'd build the box anyway, so he had to be down here, and you kept asking me where he was. It was awful. Never again, darling. No more surprises, or I shan't last till you are eleven!" "So that's what you were doing,

Dad." Laura looked over Millie's neck at him, and beamed. "And Millie seems to like it. Oh!! Thanks, Mum – and thanks, Dad." Dad seemed to have something in his eye. Her friends from school had come in too now, and Shelley and Janet. Laura looked round at them all, at her family, her friends...and her very own beautiful dark bay Shetland pony.

Next...

Millie's Magical Christmas

The Saturday after what Laura called her "best birthday ever", she'd just got to the stables and was filling Millie's water bucket when a familiar voice made her nearly jump out of her skin!

"Now young lady! It'll be hard work if we're going to qualify this pony for Olympia. I just hope you're ready for it!" Marching into the yard came Mrs Webb – with Mum and Dad close behind her!

"Now this pony's finally yours, you'd better not let us all down, young lady. Your Dad's done his part" – she indicated the newly built Shetland-sized stable – "and your Mum managed to get some money from somewhere. We don't know where," she laughed. "And she's not saying! But I've got a stake in all this too, so..."

Mrs Webb went onto explain that she had been on the lookout for a younger pony to train up and also a possible new jockey. She'd had been quite impressed with Laura's performance on Samba, and when a friend had considered buying Millie, Mrs Webb had looked at her too, made the connection and she and Sally had hatched the plan.

"But you've still got a lot to learn, so we'd better get to work. I'm helping with the costs – just this year, mind. I'm going to sponsor you in my father's memory. My dad was a real tough horseman and he didn't know the meaning of second best, so you'd better not let his memory down either." Her deep voice sounded as fierce as ever, "So what do you say? Give it a try?" With that, she finally stopped talking.

Laura opened her mouth to answer, then stopped and looked at her parents.

"Can I? Can I have a try for it?" She turned to Mum: "Can I Mum? Or would you be happier if I didn't?"

Mum hesitated and Dad put an arm round her: "We've come this far, I think we could manage a few more thrills and spills, don't you, Janey?"

Mum smiled and nodded and looked for her hanky.

"That's enough of that!" Mrs Webb said quickly, "So it's settled then. I've got everything you'll need, so no worries about equipment, or travel, or anything like that. I'll be in touch shortly about our training schedule. Toodle pip!" And she left as quickly as she'd arrived. Mum dabbed at her eyes again, and Laura went off to saddle up her pony.

***

Six weeks later, on the day of the qualifying show, Laura had to keep on pinching herself. She couldn't believe that this time they really were brown ears flicking in front of her. The crowd was cheering and laughing again. The ponies lined up. The flag dropped and they were off. Millie was in the middle of the pack going easily. Once round they went, and then again. She was flying the brushes, and cornering quite well. Suddenly a gap appeared as one pony decided to run out. Millie seized the opportunity. Laura didn't even have to ask her. She ducked into the space on the inside and shot over the last fence. Laura leaned up the pony's neck, gave with her hands, and they came round the final bend half a length behind a big chestnut. Millie lengthened her stride...they passed his shoulder...and won by a neck.

Millie had done it! They'd done it. They'd qualified for Olympia. They were going to London! Laura was completely out of breath, and speechless with delight. "Well, I didn't think much of that," Mrs Webb's voice brought Laura down to earth with a bump. "You were very lucky not to be carried out when that pony refused. Lot of work still to be done. Get her untacked and put a sheet on her. Come on girl, use your brain and think of your pony."

Laura was used to being told off. She knew Mrs Webb liked her really, but you had to get everything right or she gave you a bit of a hard time! Perhaps Laura wouldn't swap Mum for her after all.

***

They'd been schooling and practising hard over the last few weeks, so now Laura and Millie had a bit of a rest. They just hacked out gently, ambling through the woods, and Millie switched off completely. She put on some weight, and started to look a bit like the plain brown lump that had first come to the stables months before. But her mane and tail were beginning to thicken at last, and her coat shone, and Laura loved every inch of her.

And things at home were lovely now. Dad had finally found a job – with a carpentry firm – and declared that he'd found his niche in life at last. And Mum was back taking piano lessons herself now and was loving that too.

Then at the beginning of November, the training all started again, and now it was as if Millie had been doing it all her life. Mum and Dad actually came over to Mrs Webb's one weekend to watch them. Even Mum had to admit that they looked rather special as Millie and Laura cantered past them on the wind-swept track.

Dad glowed with pride as Mrs Webb said: "She'll make a decent jockey one day, your daughter." She turned to Mum and went on: "As for the pony, you got a bargain there! Sweet itch or no sweet itch, she's a gem."

Mum stuffed her frozen hands into her sleeves. Gem or not, this wasn't her scene. Too cold for a start and somehow she never seemed to have the right clothes on. They had been standing out in the wind for over half an hour and she couldn't feel her feet at all now. They were greatly relieved when Mrs Webb said, "That's enough for today. Let's go and get a cup of tea.

"Walk them all round and let them cool off," she called to the riders.

"Well, I think she's just about ready," Mrs Webb said to Mum as she handed her a cup of the strongest tea Mum had ever seen. Two of Mrs Webb's own ponies had qualified as well, and they certainly looked ready. And tomorrow was the first of December.

***

...And now – the Shetland Grand National!

"Remember! It's only one small case for you, and one dustbin for all your pony's stuff. That's all I've got room for, and when we get to the B & B place, you may have to sleep on the floor. OK?" Laura was so grateful that Mrs Webb had volunteered to sponsor her, but honestly, sometimes she sounded so fierce! She definitely seemed to get on better with ponies than with most people. But she was great at organising things, and it was just as well. They had to take so much stuff! Feed, tack, grooming kit, hoof oil, shampoo, baby oil (for putting round Millie's eyes), spare headcollar and lead rope, shoe polish (for boots, not hooves) – the list Mrs Webb gave Laura seemed endless. "Is this pony going to the North Pole?" Mum grumbled. "And why on earth do you need three of my tea towels?"

"We call them stable rubbers, Mum. I need them for when Millie needs a quick wipe."

"Well, just remember that other things will need a quick wipe when all this is over," Mum replied. "Things like cups and plates and saucepans. I shall expect help with the washing up in the New Year!"

For travelling, Millie had to have bandages and leg protectors. The people at the stables rallied round with these, and Sally lent her a huge tail guard that nearly came down to her hocks. Laura struggled to fasten it, amidst much laughter and mickey-taking. She ran round in circles feeling as if she'd never ever get there, but eventually Millie stood ready beside her dustbin of equipment, looking rather like a large parcel waiting to be posted.

Once they were on board, Mrs Webb's old lorry went rattling off along the street, and Mum and Dad stood waving until the tail-lights vanished round the corner.

* * *

Mrs Webb had three ponies entered and their young riders dozed in the cab, lulled by the strains of Dolly Parton and Tammy Wynette blaring from Mrs Webb's stereo. They were all worn out by the effort of getting ready. It only felt like a few minutes later when Mrs Webb shook them awake. They gazed blearily out of the cab windows. The lorry was going around Hammersmith roundabout, and almost at once, a huge sign loomed above them: OLYMPIA CHRISTMAS HORSE SHOW. As she looked up at it, Laura thought for a moment that her heart had stopped beating altogether.

* * *

After all the formalities were done with, the men on the huge rear gates finally let them all in. It was late in the afternoon and already dark. They bedded down the ponies in the portable stables, fed them, and put the bins in a row, taking care not to let their things spread out into the space next to them: this was reserved for some big German show jumpers.

Mrs Webb drove to the special car park and they found their way to the little hotel, hung up their jodhpurs, and unrolled their sleeping bags on the floor. Then they dashed back to watch the first big competition of the evening. Laura could hardly speak to anyone. She was so excited – blissfully happy and petrified all at the same time. She rang Mum and Dad as promised, but they couldn't get a word of sense out of her either. "Laura, are you all right?" Mum asked. "Mmmm," said Laura. "Laura, is Millie all right?" Dad asked. "Mm-Hmm," said Laura. So they gave up, sent a kiss down the phone, said they'd see her tomorrow and went back to their supper. In her sleeping bag later, Laura couldn't sleep. She knew she had to be up early to exercise Millie before the big horses came in, but her head was full of all the images she'd seen that day. She still couldn't believe she was here. She lay there with her eyes wide open. 'It's no good,' she thought. 'I'll never get to sleep – never!'

"Wake up Laura, the others have gone." Someone was shaking her shoulder, and not very gently! "How many times do I have to say it? Your ponies come first, and Millie needs feeding *now*!"

Oh no! Seven o'clock! She'd overslept…She leapt out of her sleeping bag!

***

Their race was due to start at eight o'clock that evening. Laura had given Millie a good long trot and canter with some of the other ponies and then later she walked her out to stretch her legs again.

Like most of the other youngsters, Laura had been in and out of the pony's box all day. Five doors down, she discovered Lorenzo, looking extremely full of himself. He must have arrived this morning. She stood admiring him, pleased to see him again. As she wandered back, she heard a voice saying: "That's not Woodhurst Millie! It can't be, unless she's wearing a wig." A long-legged boy was peering at the name card Laura had made and stuck on the door. "Don't I know you?" he asked, as she got nearer to him. "Wait a minute...Yes, of course! You worked at the stables when Lorenzo was there. I saw you watching when we tried him. He's come on since then. Dad says he'll lick the pants off this lot. Are you helping someone here?" Laura pulled herself up to her not very great height: "No," she said rather haughtily. "Millie and I qualified at our county show." She turned away and went into Millie's box. "Hey come on, don't get me wrong." He grinned at her. "I wish you luck. Well done anyway, for getting here. My name's Ed. Oh, I say," he leaned over the door and his grin widened: "Could I have some of your pony's hair restorer for my dad?" Laura relented and smiled back: "My name's Laura, and Millie's mine now."

***

As Laura stood in her silks waiting with the other riders to be announced to the crowd, she almost wished Millie wasn't hers. She was so nervous. She'd rather be riding in the woods at home, with no crowds staring at her. She felt sure they were all waiting for her to do something stupid. And Mum and Dad were out there too. She mustn't let them down now after all they'd done to make Millie her own pony!

She heard the commentator's velvet tones calling out the names of the runners, and their race numbers: "Next is number six, Woodhurst Millie; jockey Laura Jackson. Then Number seven, Woodhurst Lorenzo; jockey Edward Wilson. Oh – so there are two Woodhurst ponies in this race. Two from that highly successful Northern stud! This could turn into quite a needle match!"

Somehow the commentator's voice was scarier now than in her daydreams. The riders all walked out into the middle of the arena. All these people! And the noise and the lights! But it was too late now – Mrs Webb held Millie as Laura vaulted on. "Just keep calm," she said. "It's only a bit of fun, and it doesn't matter where you finish. Let her enjoy herself, stay on the outside and keep out of trouble. Have you seen your Mum and Dad? I gave them their tickets."

Laura stared at her dumbly.

"There's no need to be scared, they're very proud of you, you know. You deserve this pony and she deserves you. You're a pretty good jockey when you try." It was the first real compliment Mrs Webb had ever paid her. She lined up with the others. She tried reminding herself 'it's only a bit of fun', but she kept thinking about Mrs Webb's father: "He didn't know the meaning of second best," she'd said.

***

"They're under starter's orders." The voice was rising in excitement now. One of the other ponies ran back, reared up and waved its front feet in the air. Millie snorted. She'd never felt so strong in Laura's hands before.

"Please don't you rear up too, Mill!" she begged under her breath.

"Are you all right, kid?" called a voice behind her. It was Ed on Lorenzo. As he drew level with her she stuck out her chin and ignored him. She wasn't a kid anymore; she was a jockey. "They're off!" As the flag dropped it was as if Millie had been watching for it. She leapt forward, and Laura nearly fell backwards over her tail. She managed to cling on as they headed for the first brush fence. The crowd shouted their approval as a dozen small hairy bullets went flying round in front of them.

"Just a bit of fun!" gasped Laura, her words getting lost in the sound of hooves. And it was fun – for Millie. Laura had managed to regain her balance, only to lose it once more as Millie shot over the second obstacle.

"Look out!" someone shouted, and a girl on a sturdy grey

banged into them on their inside. Laura's left stirrup went flying. She was so busy trying to get it back that she completely forgot to steer Millie at the bottom of the arena. But Millie somehow knew where to go. She ducked inside two other ponies with Laura hanging on round her neck like someone on a slippery pole. The crowd shouted encouragement: "Hang on!" "Don't let go yet!"

"Only once more round!" and other helpful comments. Just as she felt she must slide under Millie's stomach, Laura felt a tug on the back of her silks. Lorenzo was upsides her and Ed heaved her back into the saddle.

Millie meanwhile kept on galloping. She didn't mind the noise, the huge crowd, or the bright lights. She didn't mind anything! She seemed to know exactly where the fences were and she flew them all. As they went over the last, she turned and dashed for the winning post. The pair passed two ponies on the run-in. There was only one in front of them now. That was the pony Millie wanted to pass most of all – the flashy palomino with the glorious mane – the one she'd had to *follow* on so many rides in the past...she really wanted to get in front of him... and...in the very last strides of the race...she did.

* * *

Afterwards, Laura tried to make out that she'd meant to cut in front of the others, turn on a sixpence and charge up over the line, beating Lorenzo by a short head. Only Mrs Webb, Ed, Lorenzo, and Millie, of course, knew she'd been completely out of control. The cheering died down, except for Dad, who made such a noise that Mum turned to the old lady sitting next to them and said: "That's it! I'm never going anywhere with him ever again!"

"Well, that was the most exciting race we've had for years," the announcer was saying. "What a finish, and what a great ride from the jockey, on what I'm told is her first visit to this fabulous show. Her first, but maybe not her last! And now, ladies and gentlemen, here to present the rosettes, it is my great pleasure to present that highly talented actress – she's a fine horsewoman herself – Miss Sylvia Graham. Miss Graham is this evening accompanied by her now equally famous and talented daughter Gwen." Oh no! Of all people! Laura couldn't believe her ears.

Sylvia came towards them with the biggest rosette Laura had ever seen. It had 'Shetland Grand National Winner' written on it in gold letters. She leant down towards Laura. "Well," she said. "I'm told I'm a good judge of a horse, but I never dreamt eighteen months ago that the gorgeous gelding I bought would be so soundly beaten by the sad brown lump from the next field. And look at her now! You've turned her into one of the fastest Shetlands I've ever seen."

Gwen, standing beside her mother, was not feeling so generous Laura could tell. Her mouth was smiling, but her eyes flashed like daggers. She took no notice of Millie at all, and Laura was happy to realise that she couldn't have cared less!

As if to prove Sylvia right, in the lap of honour after the ceremony, Millie suddenly leapt in the air and charged across the arena. Laura went straight up out of the saddle, and landed flat on her face in front of the band. The crowd applauded madly. Mrs Webb picked Laura up and dusted her down, while Millie went on trotting about with her tail up. She only consented to be caught when one of Europe's top show jumpers cantered in on his beautiful grey horse, leant right down, caught up her reins and led her out, with the cheers of the entire crowd ringing in her ears.

The Exmoor

The Exmoor

The screeching of metal, the crashing and banging, the voices shouting…it had all faded as the young colt struggled back on to his feet in the half dark. He'd no idea where he was now. This wasn't one of their usual familiar paths across the moorland and without his mother leading him he wasn't sure of… His mother. Where was she? He called quietly. Then again. And when no encouraging reply came, he started calling over and over, each cry a little higher-pitched and more frightened. He began to move uneasily back the way he'd come. Any minute she'd come trotting up to him and he would take comfort by suckling. She still allowed him to drink from her occasionally, although her belly was growing again and he'd begun to sense a change in her. As long as he could remember, she had been beside him. Her warm body sheltered him from the wind and the rain, and she stood guard over him when he lay down to rest. If other ponies tried to bully him or push him away from the tastiest pasture, his mother would intervene with a quick nip on their flanks or quarters. All the mares were fiercely protective of their own offspring. They taught them to find their way to the best areas to feed, and how to find the most nutritious plants. They knew how important it was fatten themselves up for the long hard winter to come.

The little colt's mother had begun to leave him alone more often now, though she was never more than a whinny away, and always answered when he called her. His soft curly coat was coming away in places and his mane and tail were growing longer and straighter. He was growing up, and in the security of his mother's company he was learning to forage for himself and to seek out the sheltered corners of the moor against the worst of the weather. Safe with her he was growing into a sturdy Exmoor who would start to fend for himself. But at this moment he was very young – and very anxious. His mother had been moving more slowly for the past few weeks but she'd never got completely left behind before. When the strange lights had flared in his eyes and the awful noise had begun, he had taken to his heels and fled. He thought she was right behind him, then he tripped and fell and had lain bruised, winded and confused, and he only now realised that he had no idea where she was. They had been on their own away from the herd when all the noise had begun, and now, alone in the darkness, his anxiety turned to fear and he dashed back the way he had come. All of a sudden he slithered to a halt. He snorted and sniffed the air, then approached the steep slope back down to the dark strip with extreme caution. There was a quiet and almost dream-like quality to the scene on the moorland road now – other lights and people milling about. A police car, an ambulance, and a Land Rover and trailer were all jumbled up on the grass. The colt stood silent and trembling, not wanting to be seen, and poised ready to run again. He looked down on something he couldn't begin to understand.

The police sergeant understood it only too well. "Sixteen, the oldest one is," he said grimly, "and he wasn't even driving! They nicked it in Minehead and came all the way up here to do a few wheelies and heaven knows what else. Well, they won't be doing that again in a hurry." He turned his head as the bearded man wearing a coat over his pyjamas stood up. "What do you reckon then, Mr Sharp? Put her down now? It's a fair way back to Tiverton. Think she'll make it?"

The vet hesitated. He'd a real soft spot for these Exmoors, the oldest native breed in England. But this looked bad. Yes, very bad. The little mare was in a terrible state. He paused, then bent down to his bag. Over his shoulder, the mare suddenly spotted her son in the distance, and in spite of the shock and the pain she pricked her ears and tried to give a reassuring call.

Although he didn't know why'd she made the sound, something in its tone made up Sharp's mind. He put his hand on the pony's shoulder for a moment, then said, "No. It's not good, but I've stopped the bleeding, so I'll give her a shot and take her back. If she doesn't last the journey to the sanctuary, the decision will be made for me. We've got her brand and number so we can let the owner know we've got her whatever happens." They had a glimpse of three very pale young faces as the ambulance door slammed shut and the vet watched as it trundled off into the dawn haze, blue light flashing. "Let's hope those little blighters have learned a lesson," he said harshly. "Stolen car you said? The owner won't be too pleased when he sees it again. It's pretty near a right-off. And so is this poor creature." He took his mobile phone out of his pocket and dialled his wife at home. He knew what she'd say...

"My sanctuary's here for horses and donkeys who really need rescuing. I haven't got room for any more of your patients, it would be kinder to put them down, most of them." And he thought, 'Maybe she's right. This mare is sagging at the knees and she's got a foal in there. One thing's certain, that'll be dead.'

He spoke softly, "Better get a move on, Billy." The young lad with him placed the sling under the mare's stomach and they prepared for a difficult journey. The trailer drove carefully back down the road and away from the moor. A distant cry came to the mare's ears but now she was too far gone to care. The police sergeant hesitated as if he'd heard the despair in the colt's call. He looked round but he couldn't see much in the October mist. He switched on his radio.

"Are you receiving me? RTA now cleared. Lower Moors Road open to traffic. Three juveniles to Taunton Musgrove Hospital. Various minor injuries – none life threatening. I'm off duty and off home."

He put the car in gear. "Well at least it was only a wild pony they hit this time. There's plenty of them around," he said to himself. He pushed the CD back in. "A nice bit of country and western, that's what I need, to cheer myself up!"

***

The colt stood stock-still and stared after the cars. The sound of their engines faded and still he stared along the road. He was still standing there in the morning, and when the rain began to fall towards midday. It was cold rain and the wind was getting up. He turned his backside to the weather as his mother had taught him and went on waiting for her to come back.

***

Amazingly, the mare survived. She had several deep gashes on her rump and a hairline fracture of her near foreleg, numerous lesser cuts and a lot of bad bruising down her left side – and, of course, she lost the foal – but the combination of expert care and her tough constitution kept her alive. As she started on the slow road to recovery she gradually began to lose her fear and suspicion of humans.

There are some people who can do almost anything to almost any horse, and no one quite knows why. The woman who looked after her through those terrible first days was one of those people.

Someone that horses trust. She named the mare Justine, and her husband made her swear never to tell anyone the reason. She said it was because he'd brought her to the sanctuary 'Just-ine-time' and he said it was the worst joke he'd ever heard. She laughed as she massaged the mare's neck and shoulders – "to encourage the healing process, and to let her know someone cares."

The colt, meanwhile, feared and mistrusted humans. His one brief contact with them had resulted in his mother's disappearance, so any similar sound or sighting was definitely to be avoided! As the winter drew in there were few people venturing up onto the moors, and he tried to keep away from all the hard dark strips the ponies had to cross from time to time. Especially the one where he'd last seen his mother. After the accident he stayed nearby for two or three days until thirst drove him to search for water. Beside the stream, he saw some ponies that might have been from his herd, but as he approached, a strange stallion appeared from nowhere and, running at him teeth bared, had driven him away. He also approached one or two groups of mares and foals and received much the same treatment.

At first the youngsters were quite happy to run and play with him but eventually, as the days were getting shorter, they needed to concentrate on feeding and building up reserves of fat against the lean times ahead. The mares led their offspring to the higher parts of the moor for the gorse and grasses not yet eaten and now, on his own, he followed them. Through the lengthening nights, he sought shelter with the others and sometimes was allowed to rest with them but mostly he wandered alone, still expecting, still hoping that round the next rock or over the next hill he would hear a familiar voice and see his mother trotting towards him. Two months passed and the snow now covered most of the moorland, hiding the paths and blowing into deep drifts. Without his mother to guide and warn him, once or twice he fell into these snowy traps and struggled desperately before he could clamber out. His thick winter coat had two separate layers for insulation and the distinctive whorls of his breed that directed the worst of the wetness down and away from his back and sides. This saved him from a complete drenching, but the battles to regain his feet each time left him exhausted. After one such fall he became separated from the other ponies, and on his own he didn't know how to find shelter, or even where to feed. His coat soon became dull and stary and his ribs and hip-bones were showing. Worst of all, he began to feel uninterested in life. He could easily have lain down in the snow and closed his eyes forever. But some strange small spark of determination kept him going, and he almost always slept standing up.

***

In the world of horses, the first day in January is when they all become a year older, and that's official! I don't know why, but it's the rule. So, although he didn't know it, it was a few days before his first birthday that the colt found the small holly bush. He was very weak by this time, and meandering along without looking where he was going. He brushed into the bush which was covered in snow and when this fell away, he saw the dark green leaves. He tried a mouthful. It was prickly and not very pleasant to eat, but something told him to persevere.

That holly bush lasted him two days and then he found two more. They were close to one of the dark strips he'd been avoiding since the night of the noise, but he hadn't the energy to move on again. On the fourth day he heard strange sounds, shouting and laughter, and there was more of that noise he'd never forget. Not quite the same, but loud,..and still roaring and frightening. He leapt to his feet and snorted in fear.

He looked down on another scene he couldn't understand, strange objects coming swiftly towards him. Five of them. Five motorbikes were weaving backwards and forwards across the road. The winter sun, low in the sky, was dazzling and he stood half-blinded and confused. The snow had gone from the tarmac, and the bikers were taking advantage of this to see how far they could get before the temperature dropped and the road surface froze again. They were wearing black leathers, and tinsel in silver, purple and pink was threaded through the chains on their jackets. The one girl – riding pillion – had a Father Christmas hat on top of her helmet. They were in a hyped-up mood, excited by the clear cold air, the sudden sunshine and the feeling of freedom away from family and Christmas on the telly. Here on the hillside they were in charge – they could do what they liked – they were free! The girl saw the colt and pointed. They all looked over, and then, as he turned to run, they turned their bikes to follow him. He hesitated – terrified by these strange creatures and by the noise of their machines. As they began to close in on him he panicked, spun round and ran up, back up among the rocks, anywhere to get away. The bikes ploughed after him on the rough track, their wheels skidding, then sliding and slipping, as they got onto the plateau of moorland above the road. Here the snow was not so deep, and they fanned out and surrounded the colt. He ran backwards and forwards, frantically seeking an escape route, and when one of the bikes went over sideways unseating its rider, he dashed through the gap, hurtled back down the hill and slithered across the road. His feet went from under him and he landed on his stomach, all four legs splayed out, and he turned two complete circles before coming to a stop, frozen with terror. The bikers stopped to pick up their mate, and the girl said: "That's enough. Poor thing, he's scared out of his wits."

She looked ashamed and gazed anxiously down at the colt: "His mother may be somewhere near. We'd best leave him. She'll come and get him if we go. He's not hurt." She jumped up behind her boyfriend and, more quietly now, they descended to the road and drove slowly off, Indian file, into the distance. As they went the girl looked back several times, and then she took off the Father Christmas hat and stuffed it into her pocket. She thought to herself, 'He *is* hurt, he must be, he's only young and I didn't see any other Exmoors around.'

***

She was right, there *weren't* any ponies near, and he *was* hurt. When the noise died away he somehow managed to get on to his feet. The hard road had scraped skin off his legs. They were raw and red, and his knees were bruised and grazed where he'd tried to save himself from going down. He started to limp back towards the safety of the moor but the pain in his legs stopped him near the holly bushes again. He slid down into the snow beside the largest one, and pressed against the prickly leaves to get what shelter he could.

As the sun sank low and disappeared behind the hill, it got colder, and by the morning the snow was falling again and the colt hadn't moved. There was no sun that day. The sky was full of thick flakes, which fell relentlessly, covering everything. The black strip of road disappeared, and so did the smaller rocks, the holly bushes and most of the colt. As dawn broke the next day, he hauled himself to his feet and tried to chew some of the now familiar prickly leaves, the snow on them helping to wash them down.

Something kept him standing throughout that day. Only as the frosts started to bite again did his legs fold under him, and he let himself sink back onto the small bare patch of earth. Icicles from his breath formed on his forelock and whiskers, his head drooped until his nose was on the snow. His wounds had ceased to hurt and his limbs were numb. A less determined yearling would have been dead by now.

***

Away from the moors, in a small house on the edge of the nearby town, Wendy was changing to go to a party with her mates. She couldn't decide what to wear. Nothing looked right. She looked awful. Her hair was awful, her nose was too big, and her eyes were too small. 'So much for trying not to get moody and depressed,' she thought. 'So much for learning to put up with how I look, and make the best of it! I look awful! I am awful!! I'll never get a job looking like this.' She'd felt bad all day, and last night. She pushed her black curls onto the top of her head and tied them there. Then she pulled the scrunchie out again and shook her head wildly. That picture – she couldn't get that picture out of her mind: a young pony spinning on the hard road and staring at her, eyes enormous with fear. Wendy had ridden for most of her sixteen years, and only given it up when she'd started going to discos and parties, and boys began to seem more interesting than ponies. She'd not thought much about horses since. But when she'd been small she'd ridden an Exmoor mare for some friends. She'd done all the lead rein stuff, then first ridden, jumping, gymkhanas, everything really. It had been a great partnership, everyone said so, and she and Velvet had had some wonderful times together... The picture of the colt came back again, stronger than ever... But Darren didn't know anything about horses – or care about them! His bike was his pride and joy, and she had to share his enthusiasm or not see him at all. And she wanted to see Darren – a lot. She'd decided she was going to teach him about animals. After all, he'd got a dog. Slade was a lurcher cross, and he was lovely. But that was the only animal Daz had ever known. So he wouldn't have realised that the little colt would be so badly scared by them driving after him. Daz wasn't really unkind, she knew he wasn't, just showing off to impress the others, and with five of them there she'd not been able to stop them. She shook her head again to get the picture out of her mind. It was no good. The pony was still there every time she closed her eyes. He was still there, splayed out and terrified. What if his mother didn't find him? What if she wasn't around? What if she was dead?

Wendy dialled a number on her mobile.

***

Darren wasn't used to getting up early – nor was he used to leaving a party after only two lagers! But he'd never seen Wendy so determined. He secretly liked a girl to boss him about, although his dad let his mum go too far sometimes, and when *he* got married he wouldn't stand for stuff like that... Not that he was thinking of marriage to Wendy, but he did like her – a lot. So when she'd gazed at him so solemnly last night and asked him to help, he'd found himself agreeing. The people who used to own Velvet had moved to a smaller house and they didn't have any horses now, but Mr Marsh had kept his old Land Rover. He did some off-road rallies, and enjoyed racketing about in it, so when Wendy phoned he'd readily agreed to take to the moors in search of the colt. Mrs Marsh came too, clutching a box of sandwiches, several flasks of hot soup and some thick blankets.

"You can't be too careful," she warned Wendy. "I always like to be prepared for the worst. We'll be glad of something hot inside us if we get stuck!"

"We'd better not get stuck for long, Jean old girl," Mr Marsh grunted. "We've got an important appointment at the airport, don't forget." "As if I would, you old silly!" she chuckled as they all bundled into the Land Rover.

In the back they had a bale of straw, a water container and

bucket, a slightly smelly old turnout rug and some hay. In her pocket Mrs Marsh also had a home-made herbal remedy with special salts in. She was a great believer in 'salts' for recovery. "Oh if only we'd kept our old trailer, John. I knew it'd be needed one day." "Don't be so daft woman, it would have fallen apart by now. Anyway, Bill's got the one he uses for his goats. That'll be big enough. That is, if we ever find this poor little chap." Wendy watched the windscreen wipers moving the snow backwards and forwards across the screen. Was it getting lighter outside? The Land Rover had chains on its wheels and it felt very safe as it crept over the snow and up on to the moor. But they were going very slowly!

* * *

"Turn left here," said Daz. "We went up a small road that goes over the top there and the pony was on our left. We went up a track. It's before you get to that big pile of rocks, the ones that've rolled out down the slope, bit like a bag of marbles that's been spilt."

Wendy turned and looked at Daz in surprise. She didn't know he thought of things like that, but they were like marbles. Huge marbles. He was right. "It's nearly two days since he fell. How long could he survive?" She hadn't realised she'd spoken her thoughts out loud. She felt it was her fault somehow. She was suddenly tearful again and scrubbed her nose with her sleeve. Mrs Marsh looked at her kindly. She liked Wendy. She'd been pleased to hear her voice on the phone last night, though not very pleased to hear what the bikers had been doing. Pity she'd got mixed up with them, she should have stuck to horses. Pity little girls had to grow up and start fancying boys. This 'Daz' was he called? Surely that was a soap powder, not a name. He looked a real roughneck. And to terrorise a wild pony like that...and as for that dog, a hooligan if ever she saw one! Still, this Daz was here with them, willing to help, that was something. And he was the only person who knew where to start looking.

***

The colt let his head drop. He didn't really feel so cold now, just very sleepy. He was covered in snow, except for his head, and that too was soon just a white shape on the ground. He thought he could feel his mother beside him and he began to feel almost content...

Suddenly, the feeling was shattered by *that* noise again. He felt too tired to raise his head but his ears twitched and his nostrils flared. It wasn't very near, the noise, so he lay very still and waited. He hardly moved a muscle, and after a while it went away again...

***

The Land Rover had reached the place where Wendy and Daz had last seen the pony. Mr Marsh switched off the engine and they clambered down on to the snow. The flakes had stopped falling so at least they could see where they were going. Slade bounded about excitedly pouncing on imaginary enemies and barking. Wendy was confused. It all looked so different. Was that where he'd fallen and spun round? All the shapes had changed, and where was the track? That low tree looked vaguely familiar. But which way had he gone? The Marshes set off to the right of the road, about fifty metres apart, calling to each other to keep in touch, and Daz and Wendy did the same on the other side. They went one each side of the holly bushes – not very close to them – and they passed by the small shape lying there without a second glance.

They went up on to the plateau and looked as carefully as they could in the gullies and round the 'marbles'. They scrambled back down, this time even closer to the small bump in the snow, and back into the Land Rover. A little further up the road Mr Marsh stopped again, and they all did the same thing.

***

For a couple of hours they went on searching, and they were getting cold and weary when Mr Marsh said, "This is pretty hopeless Wendy. There are no hoof prints, no droppings to follow. The snow's covered it all. He could be anywhere."

Wendy's face was very pale and her eyes filled with tears.

"He could be back with his mother," Mrs Marsh added hopefully and put her arm round the girl's shoulders. "We won't give up just yet, love, but I think we all need fortifying," and she opened an enormous thermos and handed round some soup and sandwiches.

Wendy had thought she wasn't hungry, but the chunky vegetable soup was so delicious she gladly accepted a second cupful.

"Jean, you've done us proud again," declared Mr Marsh as he tucked in to one of her doorsteps. "And these pickled onions are scrumptious in a sarnie!" "Where's Slade?" asked Daz, through bulging cheeks. "That's odd. He can usually hear a sandwich bag rustling at two hundred metres."

It was then that they heard the barking. Distant barking, but excited and insistent.

"He's found something," said Daz. "That's his 'I've-got-a-rabbit-cornered' bark!"

"It sounds like he's back down near the marbles," said Mr Marsh. "Come on!" Everyone leapt back into the Land Rover, and Mrs Marsh only just had time to rescue the thermos!

***

They saw the snow flying before they saw the colt. Slade was digging furiously and only stopped when the pony, shocked into action, suddenly raised his head and stared straight at the dog's nose. Slade shot backwards and closed his mouth. This was a rather larger rabbit than he had bargained for. When Daz called him, he dashed thankfully back to his master and out of danger. Mrs Marsh and Wendy approached the colt very carefully. He struggled to rise but he was too weak. His ears went back and his eyes rolled as Mrs Marsh slipped a simple halter on him and gently made it secure.

"I think we're only just in time," she said. She beckoned her husband and Daz to bring the straw. She shook some out and began to tuck it all round the pony's frozen limbs. They dried his back and head as much as they could, put two warm blankets on him and then laid the rug over the top. They offered him water and left some hay by his nose. Wendy had pulled out her phone and the men were sorting the Land Rover out, so while it was quiet Mrs Marsh dropped a bit of her recovery mixture on to her hand and held it to the pony's lips. Amazingly, he sniffed it and licked up a little. Afterwards she always swore that her 'salts' had saved him

"We'll go back and get Bill's trailer," said Mr Marsh. "Yes, and quick too," said his wife. "We must get him out of the cold before it starts snowing again. He won't last another night...he'll be all right in the trailer for now, but we'll need somewhere for him long term. In all the excitement I'm forgetting we've not got stables any more! Oh dear oh dear, whatever shall we do?" Her jolly face was wrinkled with anxiety as she gazed at the young creature on the ground. Daz walked round from the back of the Land Rover, Slade creeping cautiously after him. "I know someone who might let us use a barn. But I'll have to go and find him – he won't be at home today."

He took a step nearer the pony, and this was too much for Slade, who jumped hastily up into the safety of the vehicle. The Marshes and Daz followed the dog in. But Wendy shut off her phone and announced: "I'm staying here. I was the one who caused all this. I can't leave him now. I've just told Mum I won't be back 'til later." "Oh, Wendy!" Mrs Marsh looked horrified. "Oh no, we can't have that. Whatever would your mum say, if we left you out here in this weather?" For an answer, Wendy picked up the spare blankets and moved slowly towards the colt. "John, do something," wailed Mrs Marsh. "Tell her not to be so foolhardy!" "What good would that do?" he turned to her and shrugged. "Surely you remember how stubborn she can be where ponies are concerned."

"All right, Wendy," he called, "we'll take Daz to find this friend and pick up Bill's trailer as we go. We won't be more than an hour. Just make sure you stay put! The skies are getting brighter all the time, and you've got blankets and all your waterproofs, so I suppose it's OK." Mrs Marsh butted in: "Here's the rest of the soup. Now, keep well wrapped up! And don't move from here whatever happens! I don't know what your mother would say...so p'raps I'd better not tell her for the moment!"

Wendy smiled at her. Mrs Marsh had always understood about ponies...and things.

* * *

Daz was thinking fast. Nippy – the biker who'd fallen off in the snow – had a smallholding not that far from the edge of the moor. Well it was his dad's actually, and it was run down and a bit overgrown, but there was a barn-type building on it and Wendy had already asked him last night if they could use it if they found the pony. When the Marshes dropped Daz off in town, he had his fingers crossed that Nippy would be playing snooker with a mate, and breathed a sigh of relief when he found him. "Well as long as my old man don't find out," Nippy said, looking round nervously in case anyone else was listening. "He'd skin me if he knew. He's got no time for people fussing about animals. I mean, he never goes out to the place now, or does anything with it, but you know what he's like – dog in the manger! Let's go and see if it's fit for anything to live in. I'll do what I can with it – just don't tell my dad!"

He put his cue back in the rack, and buttoned up his anorak against the wind as he started his bike. Daz jumped up behind him. He grabbed Nippy's collar, pulled it rather tight and said, "Nobody else knows about this. We don't want any coppers or other busybodies sticking their noses in, do we Nip?"

He tweaked the collar again and Nippy's eyes popped a bit as he quickly answered, "No, Daz, course we don't."

Daz grinned and patted Nippy on the shoulder.

***

Wendy felt a moment of anxiety as the Land Rover went out of sight, but she pulled her waterproof hood back over her head, pulled the waterproof trousers well down over her wellies and sat down on the straw beside the colt. She put herself between his head and the wind. He lay still, eyes half closed, shifting his weight occasionally from one side to the other. She was glad to see him move like this, but she remembered someone saying that once a horse went down and stayed down, its chances of survival were slim. She tried to look at his damaged legs, but he got so distressed she stopped. She tucked her gloved hands back inside her sleeves and pulled the blankets around her. They stayed like this for about half an hour, and then she gradually reached out a hand again. This time he didn't try to pull away, so she quietly stroked his forehead and ears. Velvet used to love anyone doing this – it had seemed to send her into a trance. So, Wendy rubbed the colt's forehead very gently with a circular motion, and to her amazement and delight he gradually let his nose drop until it was resting on her knee. She shifted, ever so slowly, nearer and nearer, until they were both tucked under the turnout rug, and she closed her eyes, too, as she added her warmth to the little colt's body. A ray of watery sunlight came over the hill and shone on the two of them huddled together.

***

Mrs Marsh and Slade were at the barn. She'd been supervising Nippy as he staggered about with bales of hay and straw. She was changing her opinion, *slightly*, about Wendy's new friends. They certainly weren't quite as bad as they looked – though she didn't think she'd ever get used to that ring through Daz's eyebrow! Or Nippy's terrible tattoos! She was trying not to stare at them, when Nippy suddenly asked: "Do you need any more help, Missis? Only I've got a fiver riding on that game of snooker, and I was on a winning streak when Daz dragged me away."

She had hardly opened her mouth to say "No thank you,

we're fine" before he'd legged it over to his bike and roared off. He wasn't too keen on hard work like that. And he didn't want to get involved with any horses!

***

Daz insisted on coming back to get Wendy. Bill the goatman was with them as they towed the trailer over the brow of the hill. Mr Marsh had his camera on the dashboard shelf and he couldn't resist taking took a photo of the pony and the girl sitting there together in the snow. For a moment he almost felt it would be a shame to disturb them, but already the air felt colder and it would be getting dark soon. " Don't be such a sentimental old fool, John Marsh," he told himself. "If this pony's to survive there's no time to waste." They parked the trailer as close as they could, and then, folding the rug carefully and laying it flat, the four of them managed to roll the pony on to it, so it was under his belly and ribs. Then they quickly pulled up each end, and gradually got him to his feet and supported him across the snow to the ramp. It wasn't easy. The colt struggled and showed there was still plenty of life in him, and they had to dodge a couple of flying hooves, but Wendy hung on to his head and tried to calm him as best she could. In the end, in his frozen state, they were too strong for him, and he found himself, shaking and bewildered, but safely in. The trailer was low but plenty wide enough for him, and he instinctively braced himself in the deep straw when he felt it moving underneath him.

Bill the goatman laughed as Mr Marsh drove very slowly down the track. "What a handful.

I'll stick to my girls, thank you very much! They're much more friendly – and more useful." He thought this was all a bit of a wild goose chase and he wasn't sure you were supposed to move wild ponies anyway, but he had to agree that those wounds were nasty and if they got infected the little fellow might not survive. Also his daughters had been pony-mad...so he decided to keep quiet. They took over half an hour to drive to the barn.

It wasn't that far, but there were loud bangs and bumps from the trailer, and twice Wendy made them stop so she could go and check all was well. While she'd been sitting with him, she'd secretly named the colt Bambi, because in the film he, too, had fallen and slid on the ice. But by the time they got there she thought she'd better rename him Thumper! Daz dragged open the dilapidated gate and they bounced over the rough ground to where Mrs Marsh was waiting. The barn was quite large. The wood panelling around three sides was a bit rotten in places but at one end was a breezeblock wall about six feet high, and most of the roof was still on. They'd made that corner into a sort of stable with lots of straw and some strong hurdles lashed together to keep the pony in. There was an old sheep trough, low to the ground, full of water. "Slade helped me clean that," Mrs Marsh laughed, "and then he drank most of it" They backed the trailer right up to the makeshift door, so when the ramp came down the only way for Thumper to go was into the safety of the straw-filled stable. He staggered slightly, then got his balance and turned defiantly on his captors, his front feet planted in the pile of hay that was ready for him. Mrs Marsh and Wendy spoke together: "We must leave him alone now."

They smiled at each other, both glad to see someone else understood the pony's feelings. He needed time to recover and rest. Everyone moved away, as Mr Marsh tied up the door securely with baler twine.

Mrs Marsh thought that the hay would be the safest food for now. "We don't want to give him colic on top of everything else, now do we?" she said, gazing back at him anxiously. "And we'll have to bathe those legs later too, if he'll let us. Oh dear, it'll take time for him to settle, and would you believe it we're off to New Zealand the day after tomorrow to see our first grandchild. Our son's been out there nearly four years now. We must be careful or we could easily give him colic with strange food – oh, the pony that is, not our grandson. He was born on Christmas Eve, little soul. He looks lovely – our grandson that is, not the pony – so they'll be calling him Nicholas, Nicholas John after Mr M. bless his little heart." Wendy thought to herself, 'How does she manage to say so much without stopping to take a breath?' Her dad had once said that when Jean Marsh got going she could talk the hind leg off a donkey, and Wendy, had to agree with him!

But Mr Marsh was quite used to this and he could see their New Zealand trip disappearing over the horizon, the way his wife was eyeing the little Exmoor. He interrupted her firmly: "Now you calm down Jean, you're getting all of a do-dah. This pony's safe now. We'll come back later and you can sort him out, then Wendy and Daz will take over and everything will be fine."

He was gently moving her towards the Land Rover. "She looked after Velvet often enough didn't she," he reminded her. "Now, how about looking after me and taking me home for my dinner?"

"Oh he's just like Velvet round the eye," his wife crooned," Don't you think so Wendy? Oh, just look at him."

"Yes well, maybe young Nicholas is going to be just like me round the eye," said Mr Marsh, "And you and I are going off to find out, aren't we? And we haven't finished packing yet. Come on. Leave him in peace. He's strong, Jean, or he wouldn't have lasted this long." He manoeuvred her, still talking, into the Land Rover, and the grown-ups drove away.

***

Now Slade whined softly and Daz undid the rope Mrs Marsh had used to keep him out of the way. The dog walked across, looked in through the hurdles at the colt and wagged his tail gently. "Well, Slade's given him the OK after all," Daz said. Wendy turned and gave him a hug. "Thanks for coming with us," she said. You get off home and I'll stay here with Thumper."

"You what? Wha'd you call him?"

"Thumper." "Oh well it's as good as anything I 'spose. Are you gonna spend all your time 'ere now then? Will I have to come 'ere to see you?"

Wendy looked squarely at Daz. "Yes," she said. "For a while. 'Til I know he's really OK, and we decide what to do next. That all right with you Daz?" "Will have to be I 'spose. Good job it's not too far. Next thing is, you'll have me in training or summat, but don't get any ideas about rescuing more ponies, all right? Bloomin 'orses!" he grumbled. "Thought you'd got over them." But he was grinning as he set off down the track. He liked a girl who did her own thing, and he liked Wendy a bit more every day.

Slade loped off behind his master, and Wendy went back into the barn. She quietly undid the hurdle, went in, and fastened it again. She sat down beside the wall, taking care not to crowd the colt. He moved back at her approach until he was right in the corner facing her suspiciously. She realised that the closeness they'd shared a couple of hours ago was unlikely to occur again. This was a wild pony and here he was out of his element, disturbed and fearful. Any dreams she'd had while huddled under that rug of riding him – for she wasn't very tall and Exmoors are strong and well up to carrying weight – of winning mountain and moorland classes and even qualifying for top honours with him, they were just a silly fantasy. Her job was to repair the damage she still felt responsible for, to feed him up and return him to his natural domain. But she didn't want to think about that just yet. He was so lovely, the stocky shape, that lovely colour and those gorgeous eyes. Mrs Marsh was quite right: he did look rather like Velvet. Who knows, maybe they came from the same stock?

"Thumper," she said quietly, "I'll get you better, don't you worry, and then I'll get you back where you belong." She dialled home to tell them she was staying with a friend for the rest of the evening. It was almost exactly true...

***

It was quite warm in there out of the wind, and this time she fell properly asleep. She awoke a bit later to a familiar sound. A pony munching something! She opened her eyes. He was eating the straw. The hay had been ignored but the water was definitely down in the trough. She breathed a huge sigh of relief and got quietly to her feet. Suddenly Thumper looked up and started to shake. In a moment she heard it too. A car engine. She looked at him, so tense and frightened. 'Something else must have happened to him before we chased him,' she thought. 'Surely we didn't make him as bad as this.' The hurdle moved and Mrs Marsh came in clutching several plastic bags and a bucket and another bag of sandwiches.

It was a bit of a struggle to get him to stand still, but eventually she and Wendy managed to clean up his legs a bit and squirt some purple spray onto his wounds.

"They're thinking about healing already, but this will help them along," said Mrs Marsh, slipping a few more of her salts into his water. "And that spray's good too. We'll give him a handful of milk pellets now. See how he goes. We've got a whole day before we have to fly off, but if he's not much improved by tomorrow night, we'll have to think about getting the vet..."

Wendy clutched her arm: "Then it'll all come out about how we chased him and everything," she gasped, "and the boys'll get into trouble…and they'll take Thumper away. I can get him better. I'll stay with him here 'til he's OK. Please Mrs Marsh. Don't tell anyone else, not yet." As if the colt was on her side he did eat a few of the milk pellets after a while. He didn't seem to know what to do with them at first, so Wendy went outside, found a few bits of grass and mixed them with it, and that did the trick.

"Well, if you just keep him eating, and keep him quiet," Mrs Marsh said, smiling at Wendy. "Then *maybe* no-one else need know for the time being. Not 'til he's recovered. But then you must tell the authorities, my dear. He's not ours, is he? Come on now, I'll take you home. You come back in the morning. He'll be fine 'til then."

She turned and put her hand out to the colt. Thumper let her pull his ear gently. He was too busy with the straw to mind.

***

Wendy now spent most of her days at the barn. Thumper had got used to her, and to the buckets of food. He tucked into the straw too, and hadn't lost any more weight, so Mrs Marsh had allowed herself to be taken to the airport, leaving behind a long list of instructions – and a plastic bottle of her mixture.

"Now don't you forget Wendy," she'd said, "two teaspoons twice a day. He likes it now. I always knew he would. Isn't it strange, animals seem to know what's good for them, better than we humans do half the time. I was only saying the other day..." Her voice faded away, and Wendy waved, as Mr Marsh drove off, with all their cases and a very large blue teddy bear in the back.

Thumper would now stand and let Wendy bathe his legs and they started to heal quite well. But he didn't much like anyone else, especially men. He seemed to hate Daz's deep voice, and the noise and the smell of his bike. Wendy made him leave his machine outside the gate, and asked him never to rev up the engine close to the barn, but Thumper still wouldn't let Daz come near him. He liked Slade though, and the dog quite often went and lay down near the colt. Once or twice they sniffed each other, and it was as if a secret signal passed between them – some animal secret that only they knew about.

The colt became stronger and started to feel well again. He grew more adventurous and began to move around inside the barn. Wendy and Daz had cleared it all out and he now had the whole space and the hurdles only blocked the main doorway.

He could work up quite a speed, starting from the corner where his bed was, and swinging round in a big circle. After a couple of near misses he learned how to avoid the four wooden posts that held up the roof. Slade had lost all fear of the colt and sometimes Wendy found them playing chase together around these posts. Thumper was quick, but the dog was quicker. He could turn at speed without losing his legs from under him, and the little pony was always the first to run out of steam.

Then Wendy might find him standing near one of the cracks in the wooden wall, sniffing at the air. Was he contemplating freedom? How much longer could they keep him away from the moor? And how would they get him back without other people finding out? She could sit for hours just watching him, seeing his confidence returning and his tough little body regaining its shape. His ribs didn't show so much now, and his cuts and grazes were healing. She loved him and she couldn't imagine what she'd done with her time before they'd rescued him.

* * *

Nippy was quite taken with Thumper too. Because Daz had to go to work several miles away, Nippy often gave Wendy a lift out to the barn being careful to park by the gate and not to rev his bike when he got near, and once or twice he'd walked up to peep in at the pony, when she was too busy to notice. He watched the mad chase around the pillars one day, and was amazed that either of the animals survived it. Nippy thought to himself, 'It wouldn't be bad to be a wild horse – you could really get some speed on. Nobody would be able to catch you and whack you one like my dad does sometimes.'

He'd been sworn to secrecy, and he never meant to tell the others, but at the end of the second week he went down to the pub for the usual Friday night with the lads, and, what with the darts and the skittles, not to mention the beer, he found himself telling them all about it. He woke in the morning with a headache – and a guilty conscience.

He'd promised Wendy not to talk. Oh hell, what had he done? And what would she do to him, if she found out? He took her out to the barn as usual and without waiting for her to disappear inside he fled.

Wendy went into the barn. Slade was there already. He'd taken to coming over from Daz's house and staying with Thumper each day. She fed the pony as usual. She'd washed his feed bowl and was clearing the droppings when Thumper suddenly started snorting. His ears shot forward, then flat back, and he started shaking again. She recognised the signs and knew he must have heard a car, but who could it be? Then Wendy too heard the noise. Not a car, but the roar of several bikes – coming fast. She ran to the doorway in time to see Spike, Del and Masher, and a couple of others that she didn't recognise, skidding to a halt right outside the barn, revving their bikes madly before jumping off. The noise again, coming so close, then all these people with their awful smelly machines – it was too much for Thumper. He turned his back on the approaching figures and hurled himself at a place in the wall where some of the wood had fallen away and a large patch of light showed through. He jumped, he scrabbled, his forelegs got over, his tummy followed, but then he was stuck. He struggled frantically, legs flailing, but the broken timbers were hurting him and he suddenly felt weak and unable to move. He gave up and hung there, half in and half out of the barn, stranded like washing on a line. The bikers stared in consternation. Masher laughed, but it was a nervous laugh. "Oo no," said Del. "Wendy'll kill us! Oh no, stupid thing, what do we do now?" "You'll help me get him down, you thoughtless blooming idiots." Wendy felt like smacking their silly grinning faces, and her anger wiped their smiles away. "You've nearly killed him once," she cried. "Do you want to finish the job this time? Come on and help him." She dashed outside and the bikers followed in embarrassed silence. "Come with me," she said. "Just do what I say and maybe nobody else'll get hurt." She tore off her sweater and walked quietly up to Thumper.

"Steady boy, good boy. I'll get you down, good boy."

She reached up and deftly dropped the jumper completely over his head.

"Oh that's what they do with race horses when they won't go in them stalls," Masher said loudly. "I've seen it on the telly." At the sound of his voice Thumper started struggling frantically.

"You idiot," Wendy hissed. "He'll really hurt himself in a minute. Why don't you grow up? Grow up, and shut up." She glared at him furiously again – and Masher shut up. Wendy grabbed hold of the jumper to keep it in place and talked quietly to the terrified animal. When the pony was still again she whispered fiercely, "Now, you lot put him up there, so you can help get him down. Let's hope no-one gets killed doing it! Two to each front leg. Get round here Masher and Del, and you two, take the other one. Don't touch him 'til I say, then lift and push him backwards hard. Good boy Thumper, good boy. It's OK, it's OK. I'm here, I'm here...Push," she shouted, "Now!" The lads lifted and pushed hard. They were too quick for Thumper. He didn't have time to struggle – luckily for them. And then he was free, back in the barn. The sweater flew into the air as he hurled his head about. He stood for an instant, his legs braced, his body taut as a spring, and then he whirled around and threw himself at the hurdles in the doorway. They gave way, and he took off over the weeds and ruts outside, jumping over a wheel of one of the terrible machines, out of the gate and was gone. Wendy ran frantically after him, but by the time she got to the lane there was no sign of him. "He'll be hit by a car," she wailed. "He won't know what to do, where to go. Oh he's gonna be hurt again, I know it." And she burst into sobs. "We only wanted to come and see him," Dell said. "We didn't want to 'urt him. We didn't believe Nippy. We just wanted to see for ourselves," Masher added shamefacedly. "Well I hope you're all pleased with yourselves now," Wendy shouted. "All of you, go away, and take those wretched bikes with you." They went, and she turned dejectedly back into the barn. It took her several minutes to realise that Slade was gone too. Just for a moment she nearly sat down and cried, but that would be giving up, and she wasn't going to do that. The two animals she loved most in the world needed help. She set off down the road.

"Daz will help me," she said to herself. "I must find him." And she broke into a run.

***

Thumper ran too. He ran and ran until his wind gave out. The sun was up above the hills now. He was bathed in sweat again, and the feel of the road under his hooves frightened him and brought back a sudden horrible feeling. As he stood confused and scared, a huge noisy thing appeared around the bend and bore down on him. He threw himself to one side and fell into a ditch. It was half full of grey melting snow, which broke his fall, and the lorry roared by without slowing down. Thumper was petrified. His heart was pounding and he could get hardly any air into his lungs. As he lay there another large smelly thing rattled past his face, and all his instincts told him he must get away from the dark strip that had always meant danger. But where should he go? And how could he escape the noise? As he went to raise his head, something wet suddenly slapped him on the nose. He struggled to his feet. The wetness came again, and Slade, his tongue lolling, lifted his snout and gave Thumper a final slurp across the muzzle. He walked around the colt, then turned back expectantly and waited for him to follow. Slade led the way across the lane. He slid his slim body through a gap in the hedge, and stood on the other side squeaking and whining until Thumper understood that he was to follow. The blackthorns were daunting but the pony closed his eyes and dropped his head and neck and pushed. At first it seemed impossible, but he buckled his knees and stooped low and pushed again. Still he could make little impression on the tough springy stems, until another roaring rattling monster rounded the bend in the road, and his terror catapulted him through. He lay spread-eagled on the ground for the second time in his short life. This time the surface was yielding, and although his scarred legs hurt him, there was no real damage done. He scrambled to his feet and took off after the dog as fast as his legs would carry him. Cattle stared in amazement at the strange pair moving amongst them. Slade clambered through another hedge. This one was straggly in parts and Thumper easily found a gap. They found themselves in woodland and made good progress now, picking their way carefully through the trees, though the pony stumbled over one or two fallen branches. They skirted a farmhouse and its outbuildings. A distant figure turned and looked in their direction. A hand pointed, and they heard a voice, and another figure came out of a shed. Slade barked once urgently and the pony seemed to know they must move on – and fast. They doubled their speed, slipping and sliding a little as the ground dropped away in front of them.

Crossing another two big sloping fields, they had to jump a low wire fence and at a stream they both stopped to drink. The colt would have liked to stop and graze on the rough winter grass by the water. It was a long time now since Wendy had given him his breakfast bucket. But Slade turned his head and listened, then whined and barked, urging the weary pony on. They kept up a steady trot, until, breasting another small hill, Thumper slid to a halt, and stood, hesitating. There was another dark strip in front of them and Slade moved purposefully down towards it.

The strip was wide, with white marks in the middle. The traffic was constant – cars, vans and lorries – and to cross this would surely be too difficult and dangerous. The pony stood on the hill, and Slade waited at the roadside looking back at Thumper, unsure and nervous. A familiar sounding machine came into sight, then another, and a third. Then, from the opposite direction, yet another appeared. The bikers!

***

Nippy was out looking for the missing pair. When he'd found out the lads had gone to the barn he'd followed, and met them all and heard the story. He couldn't face Wendy or Daz, so rode off in search of Thumper. He didn't know what he'd be able to do to help but he was going to try. He found a gap in a hedge that looked newly done. If they'd gone across old Jenkins's land they'd be heading towards that main road. If they got across his land at all, that was... He was known to be a funny beggar, old Jenkins. He didn't like anyone, or anything, trespassing on his precious land. And he wasn't above shooting things – foxes, rabbits, even a badger or a deer, people said. He wouldn't take kindly to a strange dog on his place, amongst his stock. Nippy turned the accelerator. His old bike rattled under him as he headed for the main road. He saw the dog at the roadside before he saw the other bikes. He slid to a stop and jumped off. The others turned across the carriageway and pulled up beside him and they all looked up to the rise where Thumper was standing.

"He'll never get over here," Del said. "He'll end up as flat as that hedgehog we just passed." "I don't fancy his chances. It's getting dark now and the cars'll never see him in time to stop," Masher took off his helmet and stuck a grubby finger in his left ear and wiggled it about. Slade suddenly moved forward onto the tarmac, and Nippy only just grabbed his tail in time as a red car swerved to avoid him.

"Get off the road, you hooligans," the large woman inside the car shouted, "before you cause a serious accident!"

"He's gonna cross in a minute," Del said. "I know this dog. We've got his mother. And once they decide to do something they don't give up 'til they've done it. Talk about stubborn!"

Nippy was standing there clutching Slade by the neck when Daz came racing up, with Wendy clinging on behind him.

Daz took in the situation at a glance and took command. "It's simple," he said. "We must just stop the traffic!" He moved out from the verge with a hand raised and was greeted by the scream of a horn as he threw himself back to safety. "Stop the traffic eh?" Spike spoke for the first time. "Well that's not much of a problem, is it!"

He spat out his chewing gum and laughed. Daz made one or two more attempts, but drivers keen to get home before the snow came down again, were not prepared to take notice of a bunch of 'Hell's Angels' looking for trouble at the roadside.

Spike spoke again: "Hey, Mash, do exactly what I do, and you Del. Come on! And you, dog," he looked down at Slade and whispered urgently: "Lie down, lie down and stay down!"

Slade looked back at him for a long moment, then did as he was told. "You, Wendy, get up that slope behind the horse, wait 'til I shout, then try and send 'im down here."

Wendy pushed through the bushes and walked in a wide circle around Thumper. He started to move back, and she spoke to him as softly and as calmly as she could. At her familiar voice he stopped and turned, but made no move towards the road.

Spike said: "If they don't want to stop, we'll have to make them." He spun his bike and wheeled it a few yards back down the road. Then he turned and stood, poised on the verge, until a gap in the stream of traffic appeared, then he dashed into the middle of the road, threw his bike down and threw himself down beside it. Daz had realised almost straight away what Spike was planning, so he ran the other way, and mirrored his friend's action, laying down his bike in the other lane of traffic. Suddenly the busy road was strewn with bikes and bodies, and vehicles screeching to a halt to avoid them. "Now Wendy. Now." yelled Daz, and she rushed towards Thumper, her arms spread and waving. He stared, bewildered by the sudden change in her, and then dashed forward wildly. Slade leapt to his feet and rushed back to the colt and snapped around his heels, urging him towards the road. People were getting out of their cars and starting to make angry noises as they saw that nobody seemed injured, or even slightly hurt. "Hurry up, you stupid little horse," yelled Spike, as a very big man got out of a van and headed for Masher with an nasty look on his face. As if the two animals had heard the urgency in his voice, they appeared behind the hedge. The dog dashed out across the clear expanse of tarmac and a moment later, the small hairy pony, ears flat back and eyes rolling with fright, slipped and slithered after him and disappeared in a flurry of hooves up the far bank and out of sight. "This is what comes of underage drinking," growled the van driver. "We ought to have the law on you lot." "There could easily have been a terrible pile-up. What on earth were you all playing at?" asked a woman in a woolly hat. Her elderly mother, strapped in the passenger seat, kept calling, "Get the police! Phone for an ambulance! Where's the AA?" "Whose dog was that?" said another man, as he checked his bumper for dents after sliding into

Daz's back wheel. "Strays should be rounded up and seen to, not left to run around and cause accidents."

He was about to demand some names and addresses, but as he straightened up again, all he caught sight of was the tail-ends of five motorbikes disappearing down the road.

"And like a fool, I never even got any of their numbers," he lamented later to his wife, as he told her of his extraordinary drive home. She turned his chop under the grill, and pretended to be listening as he rattled on: "The youth of today… I-don't-know-what's-the world-coming-to? There were dogs and ponies all over the road!"

She put some salt in the potatoes.

* * *

Once they were safely over the road, the dog and the pony slowed to a walk, and fairly soon, even though it was now getting dark, Thumper began to realise that he was on a piece of moorland that he knew. He stopped and looked around him. The snow had melted in most places and there, standing out against the bare ground, were some holly bushes, two of them almost devoid of leaves. And beside them there was a pile of old hay, and one blue glove, trodden into the ground. Slade stopped, sat down on the hay, and licked one of his back paws. He'd caught it on the fence earlier. He and Thumper looked at each other. Then the colt turned and trotted up the gully between the marbles. At the top he looked back and gave a little call. Slade's tail slapped the ground a couple of times, then he stood up, stretched himself, and sauntered back down towards the road. The colt watched him for a moment, then turned away onto the moor and disappeared into the darkness.

* * *

Thumper's mother never went back onto the moor. She'd have had trouble breeding again, and her back was damaged, so her owners weren't interested in keeping her. So she stayed as a companion to any youngsters coming into the sanctuary. And very good at her job she was too, mothering them and bossing them about. In fact the staff started to wonder how on earth they'd managed before she came. That autumn Thumper was rounded up in the drift and examined with the other ponies. The Exmoor commoners were surprised to find an unbranded colt of his age. But they all agreed he was an excellent specimen of the true native breed, and decided to leave him on the moor to pass on his bone and his toughness to the foals of the future. He gathered a few mares about him and guarded them fiercely, keeping them well away from any roads.

Wendy did get a job that year, and she did marry Daz in the end – four years after Thumper was rescued. And once in a while now, she pinches Daz's old bike and rides out onto the moor, often with a small boy strapped onto her back, but always with Slade, his nose a bit greyer now, perched in a basket on the pillion. They walk up amongst the rocks, and if they're lucky, they might see a sturdy young stallion standing near the big stones that look like spilled marbles. He sniffs the air and tosses his head, and sometimes he seems to be looking straight back at the dark-haired girl and the old dog sitting quietly above the road beside some stunted old holly bushes.